DANGEROUS LOVE

An innocent photographic assignment in Kenya with business partner Tom puts Ellie's orderly life in turmoil when she unexpectedly bumps into an old flame, Harrison Grey. He once hurt her very badly and she has no intention of letting him back into her arms. But keeping her distance from him isn't easy, and when another face from the past threatens them both, she questions her feelings for him. As they battle for survival, will their love be rekindled?

Books by Deborah Blake
in the Linford Romance Library:

CAUGHT IN CUPID'S NET

DEBORAH BLAKE

DANGEROUS LOVE

Complete and Unabridged

LINFORD •
Leicester

First published in Great Britain in 2004

First Linford Edition
published 2005

British Library CIP Data

Blake, Deborah
Dangerous love.—Large print ed.—
Linford romance library
1. Love stories
2. Large type books
I. Title
823.9'2 [F]

ISBN 1–84395–590–3

Published by
F. A. Thorpe (Publishing)
Anstey, Leicestershire

Set by Words & Graphics Ltd.
Anstey, Leicestershire
Printed and bound in Great Britain by
T. J. International Ltd., Padstow, Cornwall

This book is printed on acid-free paper

1

The hot, Kenyan sun pounced on Ellie's neck as she clambered out of the mini-bus. The two-hour journey from Mombasa airport, cooped up in the cramped and airless vehicle had left her travel-worn and she could feel the sweat trickling down the backs of her knees, and her hair stuck to her forehead in damp curls.

'Phew! I'm melting,' she said.

Tom climbed out beside her, stretching his long legs and arching his back.

'Thank goodness we're here,' he said as he pushed his fingers through his short, dark hair.

Two porters had sprung from nowhere and were pulling and dragging their luggage from the rear of the bus. Tom darted round the back after them.

'Careful,' he told them, grabbing at two canvas holdalls. 'I'll take these.

They're my cameras and I wouldn't want them being damaged accidentally.'

The porters stared blankly at him holding on to the straps of the bags.

'Kamera,' Tom showed off his Swahili, mimicking taking a photograph.

'Ah, ndiyo.'

The porter understood as he let go the straps and Tom took possession of his beloved camera and all the paraphernalia that went with it.

Ellie wandered over and stood under the bamboo canopy that framed the main entrance to the Hotel Hisani. Fanning herself with a magazine that she'd been reading on the plane she looked at the surroundings and where she and Tom would be staying for a few weeks. She couldn't believe she was actually here at last.

The porters carried the luggage ahead of them into the cool interior of the reception area. Tom was weighed down with all the photographic gear, so Ellie approached the reception desk to book in. As she opened her mouth to speak, her words were snatched away by a deep-sounding voice coming from her right.

'Miss Britten, Mr Nesbitt. We've been expecting you. Welcome. Welcome to the Hotel Hisani.'

A rather dashing, Richard Gere look-alike, wearing a very loud shirt, was hurrying forward to greet them both. A heavy gold bracelet jangled on his wrist as he grabbed Ellie's hand and kissed it, briefly nodding at Tom as he did so.

'Vince West,' he stated, 'hotel manager.'

'Very pleased to meet you.'

Ellie smiled approvingly, taking in the iron-grey hair and five o'clock shadow that gave him his movie-star looks.

'Do you always greet your guests like this?'

'Only the beautiful ones. No, any friend of Ernest's is a friend of mine. I hope you had a good journey.'

'Apart from all the potholes in the road from Mombasa,' Tom said with a laugh. 'I feel as though my insides have turned into jelly.'

'Ah, yes, the road does leave a lot to be desired. The heavy rainfall washes it away all the time, you see.'

'Of course,' Tom agreed.

'Anyway, you two both look in need of a cold drink. Come this way into the lounge. Our mutual friend, Ernest, is waiting there for you both. I hope he hasn't fallen asleep.'

Vince laughed and Tom and Ellie followed him down some marble steps into another foyer with two small offices off it to the left. Ahead of them another door revealed the TV room. To the right more steps led down to a small reception lounge that opened on to the terrace and pool area.

Ernest Grey was reading a magazine, seated on one of three large sofas that were arranged around a massive, oak coffee table. He was a roly-poly of a man, with ruddy cheeks and a dimpled chin. He took off his reading glasses and pulled himself up awkwardly as

Vince approached with his latest arrivals.

'Ellie, my dear child, how lovely it is to see you. You haven't changed at all,' he greeted her.

'Not so much of the child, Ernest.'

She shook his hand warmly and leaned forward to kiss him gently on the cheek.

'You look just the same, too. How long has it been?'

'Ten years,' he said wistfully. 'Too long, I'm afraid.'

'I was only seventeen when we last met,' she said to Tom. 'How the years fly by.'

'Don't they just.'

Ernest looked at Tom, waiting for an introduction.

'Oh, this is Tom Nesbitt, my business partner. Tom, Ernest Grey, my father's oldest friend and my godfather.'

'How do you do, Tom?'

They shook hands. Then Ernest turned to Vince.

'I think I mentioned to you that this

young pair have started an image library, whatever that is.'

'You did and it sounds very intriguing,' Vince replied. 'You must tell me more, but please, all of you, take a seat first and I'll organise some drinks.'

He disappeared off towards the bar.

'I'm so sorry about your mum and dad,' Ernest said to Ellie. 'I really miss them. I knew Roger from when we were both kids. I was very upset not to be able to get over for the funeral.'

Ellie put a comforting hand on his arm.

'Ernest, I understand. How could you when you were poorly? I wouldn't have expected you to travel all that distance. It was a comfort to me just knowing that you had organised everything from this end. I'll always be grateful for that.'

Vince returned, followed by a young waiter carrying a tray of drinks and soon they were all sipping cocktails from tall blue glasses with pieces of orange clinging to the rims. While in a lighter mood, Tom explained the concept of the new business venture that he and Ellie were setting up.

'Gradually our image library will build up into a collection of many different photos and they'll be available to a host of different clients,' he finished off.

'Who will actually want them?' Vince asked. 'Sorry, I mean, how do you intend to market them?'

'They will be available to anyone,' Tom explained. 'That's where Ellie comes in with her marketing experience. These images can be used in books, magazines, calendars, on mugs, key rings, cards. Lots of companies need images for all sorts of things but don't necessarily have the time to go and photograph things themselves. Ellie has a business plan to approach companies and explain what we have to offer.'

'Ah, I'm with you,' Vince said. 'And that is why you are over here in Kenya, to do some animal photography for your library.'

Ernest looked serious for a moment.

'Of course, but Ellie does have another reason for being here, too.'

Ellie looked sad.

'It's the fifth anniversary of my parents' death. They were killed on their yacht off this coast. I want to hire a boat and scatter some flowers into the sea, say a few words, you know. I'm hoping that might help me to come to terms with what happened — to try and understand it.'

Vince looked at Ellie sympathetically.

'Ernest has told me about the tragedy. I remember all the publicity over here when it happened. It was just before I took over the hotel. It must have been a very unhappy time for you. Perhaps you would permit me to organise a modest ceremony at sea for you. I have access to several boats. It would be a way of offering my condolences.'

'Thank you, that would be very kind of you,' Ellie said. 'It had always been my parents' dream to sail their yacht around the world and to have those dreams dashed by pirates at sea in the twentieth century, well, it just seems too unbelievable.'

'I'm afraid modern-day pirates are a very real shipping hazard. Not very common off the coast off Kenya, but not altogether unknown.'

Ellie sighed and picked up her glass again to cover up the awkward pause in the conversation. Ernest tactfully changed the subject.

'I had better get going now, let you both unpack and get settled in. How about coming over to the animal centre tomorrow? Not too soon, eh? I thought you'd want to get stuck in right away. I've got plenty planned for you while you are here.'

'That will be great, Ernest,' Ellie said, pushing the memories of her parents out of the way for the moment. 'I'm looking forward to seeing the place. How far away is it? Do we need to arrange for transport?'

'No need,' Ernest said, picking up his

reading glasses from the table and snapping them back into their case. 'All arranged,' he assured them. 'I'll come over in the morning and pick you both up. Will nine be OK? Not too early? Harrison would have come but he's tied up first thing. You remember Harrison, don't you?'

The colour drained instantly from Ellie's face.

'Harrison?' she faltered over his name. 'I had no idea he was here in Kenya with you.'

'Didn't I say in my letter?' Ernest frowned. 'I was sure I had. He's been here for several years now. He can't wait to see you.'

I'll bet, Ellie thought.

'Who's Harrison?' Tom said.

He had seen Ellie's reaction at the mention of the name and it made him feel uneasy. Ellie was at a loss for words, although Ernest had not noticed the effect it had had on her.

'My son,' Ernest said proudly. 'It may have been me who set up the Ernest

Grey Animal Centre all those years ago, but Harrison deserves his name up there, too. He has done so much for the centre over the last few years. I don't know what we'd do without him.'

'He's certainly got my vote,' Vince said. 'Great guy. He organises all the safaris for my hotel guests. They love him. I believe he has you two booked on his next trip to Moja Camp.'

Just then, the reception manager came over and handed Vince two room keys.

'Ah, your rooms are ready now and your luggage has been taken there.'

They all rose and walked back to the main foyer to say goodbye to Ernest until the next day.

Ellie walked ahead with him and as Tom lagged behind, Vince caught hold of his arm.

'I noticed Ellie's face, too, at the mention of Harrison's name,' he said to him. 'Do you think there's some history there?'

Tom shrugged.

'I've no idea, mate. She's never mentioned him before.'

'She's a great-looking woman. You two aren't an item, are you? Only, I've organised two separate rooms. Did I get it wrong?'

Tom suppressed his annoyance.

'No, you got it right. We are strictly business partners, nothing more.'

Vince raised an eyebrow in mock surprise.

Later that evening, after dinner, Tom and Ellie sat in the lounge together, drinking more exotic cocktails. A male group was playing live for the hotel guests, and the main lights were turned down low, with coloured fairy lanterns strung across the high, thatched roof. The pool glimmered outside just beyond the group and couples were moving together out on the dance floor. Tom thought what a romantic setting it was — and how he would like to take Ellie in his arms right then and move her around the dance floor close in his embrace.

It was Ellie who had approached him with the idea of the image library earlier that year. He was a photographer on the magazine she edited. He liked the idea and they had spent a lot of time and energy getting it off the ground. On Ellie's part, things had remained strictly business, but Tom couldn't help but find her attractive.

He had hoped that this working holiday would bring them closer and that maybe their relationship would take on a more intimate rôle. Now, it seemed, Harrison Grey could be a spanner in the works and Ellie's attention might be taken up elsewhere.

He stared at the long blonde tresses draped over her pale shoulders, as yet unkissed by the Kenyan sun and imagined his lips caressing her neck. Suddenly she turned and looked at him as if she had felt his eyes on her. She had drunk more than a few cocktails and her eyelids looked heavy, but instead of making her look tired she looked sultry and sexy. She held out her glass to him.

'Shall we have another drink?'

Tom's stomach muscles contracted.

'About Harrison.'

He stumbled over the name, disliking the man already.

'Did you . . . I mean were you and him an item once?'

He knew the answer before Ellie replied.

'Once,' she recalled. 'It was a long time ago. I was young and naïve, and he was a grown man who took advantage of an innocent girl, but it's all in the past. Now, shall we have that drink?'

Next morning, Ellie told herself she was over Harrison, but nevertheless dressed carefully in readiness for her encounter with him. As she put some things into her shoulder bag she dreamily recalled that night ten years ago when she had been out celebrating her eighteenth birthday.

She'd been in the Candy Shop Nightclub with friends and hadn't seen Harrison for four years as he had been away training as a vet, so when she had bumped into him at the bar, she was more than a little surprised.

'Harrison, what are you doing here? I thought you were training in the Lake District.'

Harrison had peered at her in the half-light. He'd had a few drinks and looked her up an down approvingly. He shouted back above the music.

'Ellie? Ellie Britten? Fancy that. Well, look at you, all grown up. Goodness, I haven't seen you for years.'

Not since I was a spotty thirteen-year-old with braces and puppy fat who idolised you from afar, Ellie thought.

'How are you? What are you doing with yourself these days? Finished school?'

Ellie nodded, and indicated a crowd of girls on the dance floor.

'I'm at college with that crowd. We're celebrating my birthday.'

Harrison offered to buy her a drink, then another one. He danced with her and she couldn't believe that after all those adolescent years of hero-worship, she had finally been noticed by her godfather's handsome son. He told her that he was home for a month before taking up a new post in Devon. Ellie's college was closed for the summer break so it seemed natural to spend some time together.

Throughout that lazy, balmy August the two of them became inseparable. He swept Ellie off her feet and she fell madly in love with him. She thought he felt the same. He certainly led her to believe that it was more than just a summer fling . . .

Her thoughts were interrupted by a light knock on the door of her chalet.

'Ellie, are you ready yet?' Tom's voice called.

'Just coming,' she replied and picked up her bag and a flimsy white blouse, before opening the door to him.

Tom looked at her white trousers, skimpy yellow top and tan sandals and frowned.

'Are you sure you're dressed for an

animal centre?' he queried. 'One nudge from an elephant and you'll be filthy, or are we dressing for Harrison?'

'Certainly not,' Ellie said indignantly. 'I told you, we are ancient history. He means nothing at all, but you're right, I'll get filthy. Hang on a minute, I'll change.'

Tom waited out on the veranda and Ellie joined him a few minutes later. She had substituted khaki shorts for the white trousers and replaced the sandals with safari boots.

They were silent as they followed the path from the chalet rooms round to the main bar and lounge area. Tom wanted to talk to her about Harrison but sensed she did not. It would have to wait. Ernest was waiting to take them to the centre where Tom was sure Harrison would dash all his hopes of getting together with Ellie.

2

It was a forty-minute drive to the animal centre. Tom sat in the back and tried to listen to what Ernest was saying to Ellie in case he was talking about Harrison. He didn't want to miss anything, but all Ernest was doing was pointing out all the scenery.

The road was taking them out through a major sisal-growing area that focused around the small town of Vipingo. Tom stared out of the open window and moved up closer to it trying to get some cool air as they sped on, but the air blowing in was hot, as though someone was holding a hair-dryer to his face.

The landscape eventually turned hilly and as they got nearer to the reserve, the lush green of the coral coast turned more to scrubland and the rich red of the soil became more apparent.

Tom was now sitting forward in his seat with one arm resting on the back of Ernest's seat so he could see out in front of them. As he wiped the sweat from his forehead he could see two burly Kenyans opening some large, wire gates ahead of them, and a sign overhead confirmed that they had arrived at the Ernest Grey Animal Centre.

Ellie saw Harrison at once and couldn't stop the little shiver of pleasure that ran up her spine and tickled the back of her neck. She knew that she should be cool to the point of being aloof with him after what he did to her that summer, ten years ago, but all the feelings she had thought were gone came flooding back in an instant.

The truck came to a stop in front of a long, low building, painted cream and half covered by a large, creeping shrub that produced the most exotic cerise-coloured flowers. The windows all had their shutters closed to keep out the relentless sun.

'Well, this is it, and there's Harrison,' Ernest said proudly as they all climbed out.

He led Tom and Ellie towards his son, who had his back to them and was in deep conversation with one of the local workers. He seemed oblivious to their arrival, or was ignoring them on purpose, Ellie thought. He was tall and broad-shouldered just as she remembered him and was wearing jungle-green shorts and shirt with a brown leather belt and boots. Ellie couldn't help admiring his muscular, tanned calves.

Harrison turned at last to greet them, and flashed a pair of azure-blue eyes over Tom and Ellie but gave away nothing that revealed any past intimacy with Ellie. Tom renewed his dislike of this man whose manner seemed decidedly laid-back and confident.

'Look whom I've got here,' Ernest said innocently to his son.

'Well, I never,' Harrison said, the corners of his eyes crinkling affably.

'Look at you, Ellie Britten. Long time no see.'

He gave her a brotherly kiss on the cheeks, more of a peck really.

'You're looking really great, and you must be Tom.'

Tom extended his hand.

'Yep. Tom Nesbitt, Ellie's partner,' he said cryptically.

Ellie was too busy staring at Harrison to notice Tom's rather misleading statement regarding their relationship, so failed to rectify it. She just smiled sweetly at him.

'Fancy seeing you. I was so surprised when Ernest said you were working here with him. I had no idea. After you went to start your new job in Devon you just seemed to vanish off the face of the earth.'

There was a sharp edge to her voice that Harrison chose to ignore, although Tom detected it.

'I was sure I'd mentioned it in my letters,' Ernest was saying absent-mindedly.

Ellie and Harrison were locked in eye-to-eye combat.

'Oh, Devon didn't work out at all. I moved about quite a bit for a while after that. Just couldn't settle,' Harrison told her, trying to act nonchalantly. 'I've been out here for several years,' he went on and pretended to whisper behind his hand jokingly as he added, 'Father's getting a bit old for all this now, and needs a hand.'

'Enough of the old,' Ernest said, gently scolding but obviously immensely proud of his son. 'Come on, let's get out of the sun for a bit and have some refreshments before your tour of the place.'

They made a move towards an arched entranceway, also festooned with exotic blooms. Tom sensed Ellie's hint of animosity towards Harrison and decided that whatever their history was, their parting may not have been mutual, and it was fairly obvious to him that Ellie still had feelings for the man.

After a cool drink, Ernest and Harrison took Ellie and Tom around the centre, explaining all about their conservation work there and Tom used up quite a few rolls of film, especially on the orphaned animals in the baby unit.

It was an interesting visit, with great photo opportunities but Ellie's mind was only half focused. She couldn't actually believe how calm she was, chatting to Harrison like old friends, and asking him sensible questions about the animals, when really she just wanted to slap his face and ask him what on earth he was playing at.

Even when Tom was busy with his camera and Ernest was out of earshot, Harrison did not seize any opportunity to mention their past together, not even a hint of an apology for dumping her in such a cowardly way, nor even an attempt to explain his callous actions. It was as though they were just old friends.

How could he behave as though

nothing had ever happened between them? Didn't he realise what he had meant to her? Was he totally unaware that she had fallen in love with him that summer, ten years ago? She had been so naïve that she had really believed that he had felt the same way.

She suddenly felt embarrassed as she remembered how she had given herself to him so completely, telling him all her secrets and longings. He had been her first love. She had trusted him and he had betrayed her.

When she had gone back to college and he had gone to Devon to take up his new post he had promised they would keep in touch. They had been so happy together she had been convinced that it was not the end of a holiday romance. She had been certain that their love would last and no amount of miles between them would change that. She remembered that he had said she was very special.

What a fool she had been! He had never even phoned, hadn't replied to her Christmas card. Then, not long after her Valentine's Day card to him had been ignored, on a particularly wet and windy day her father had come home one day and said, 'Oh, I heard from Ernest today. He sends his love. Oh, and Harrison is off to Thailand tomorrow with his latest flame. Lucky blighter.'

It was only then that she had admitted to herself that he was gone and he wasn't coming back to her. It had taken a long time, but she had finally got over him. And now, here he was again, standing right beside her. As she recalled their time together her stomach knotted with a sudden need for him and she couldn't make the feeling go away.

'What do you think then?' Ernest said.

He was stroking a little patch of tufted black hair on the head of one of the orphaned baby elephants.

'Isn't he gorgeous?'

Ellie caught Harrison's eye again but

quickly turned away and smiled at Ernest.

'He's lovely,' she agreed. 'Has he got a name?'

'Toupee,' Ernest said, laughing.

'Very appropriate,' Ellie replied as Tom kneeled down in front of the cute, little creature and attempted to take a close-up without the elephant trying to curl its trunk around his camera.

Later, Ernest organised for them to be driven back to their hotel. They were both silent in the late afternoon heat as the truck shook its way back towards the coast.

'You still love him, don't you?' Tom said finally.

'No!' Ellie said, too quickly, looking out of the window and sighing deeply. 'Maybe . . . oh, I don't know.'

She looked at Tom.

'It wouldn't make any difference anyway,' she continued. 'He walked away from me ten years ago without one word of explanation, and no contact since. Not exactly the actions of a man in love.'

'Have you said anything to him about it today?'

'No. I didn't really get an opportunity. Besides, he didn't say anything to me. It's as though we never happened. He should have said something to explain. Anyway, he didn't. That speaks volumes, doesn't it? So, I think I'll just leave it at that, if you don't mind. I don't want to get hurt all over again.'

'So you won't be walking around with a face like a wet Sunday for the next few weeks?'

Ellie smiled at him.

'No, most definitely not.'

There was a barbecue at the hotel that night. Ellie was refreshed after having had a nap and a shower, and she was determined to enjoy herself and forget about Harrison for a few hours.

By the time she wandered down to the main lounge area, Tom had already sampled a fair bit of the local brew and was talking to Vince at the bar. He'd caught the sun that day and already his face was looking quite tanned.

There was a large, metal hoop suspended from the ceiling over the bar inches from Tom's head and swinging precariously from it, its orange feet gripping the wire tightly, was a plump red and green parrot. It wasn't real, but hand-carved in wood by local craftsmen. There were others dotted throughout the hotel.

Underneath this particular one was the entertainments board, propped up against the wall beside the bar. It was written crudely in chalk, announcing the barbecue that night.

'Hi, Ellie,' Tom said, smiling at her as she approached, looking radiant in a flowing turquoise and pink dress and white mules. 'What can I get you?'

'I'll have one of those lovely cocktails we had earlier,' she decided, nodding a greeting at Vince. 'Good evening, Mr West.'

Vince took her hand and kissed it for the second time since her arrival.

'Call me Vince,' he said. 'You enjoyed

your day at the animal centre, I hear,' he continued.

'Very much,' Ellie said wondering whether he and Tom had actually been discussing the day or her and Harrison and she suddenly felt a bit exposed. 'So, where's this barbecue?'

It couldn't be far off as there were cooking smells wafting up over the wooden rails that bordered the decking area of the lounge.

Vince pointed at some steps that wound down away from the hotel towards the beach.

'It's all happening down there. Just make your way down and help yourself whenever you like.'

A waiter passed them and Vince called out to him.

'Jacob! Excuse me, Tom, Ellie, I've got to see to something. I'll join you both a bit later. My baby sister is coming along shortly, too. I'll introduce you to her.'

He caught up with the waiter, and Tom and Ellie took their drinks and started down the steps. People were passing them coming up with plates loaded with steaming cuts of meat and piles of potatoes and salads.

The steps wound halfway down the side of a small cliff and were covered with a primitive canopy that was entwined with more fairy lanterns and bits of shrubbery.

It opened out on to more decking overhanging the creek where five cooks were cooking mountains of meat on several large barbecues that looked like oil drums cut in half. Another table was laid with a variety of vegetables and salads. There were some tables and seats dotted about, and some people were eating there, while others were taking their food back up to the lounge area.

'I suppose some people want to be available for seconds,' Tom said, as they joined the queue.

'I'm not surprised. Look at the choice. You wouldn't be able to fit everything on one plate.'

They took their food back up to the lounge and when they'd found a table, Tom went off to get more drinks. The group started playing again. Later, as the waiters cleared away their plates, Ellie looked up as Vince approached their table, a blonde girl hanging on to his arm.

'May we join you?' he enquired, scraping back chairs and sitting down as Ellie nodded.

'This is my baby sister, Cameo,' Vince said. 'This is Tom and Ellie, babes.'

'Hi, everyone,' Cameo said from underneath a mop of short blonde curls.

She was wearing sunglasses on top of her head and big gold earrings.

'Are you guys enjoying yourselves?'

'Hi, yes, it's lovely,' Ellie assured her. 'Your brother has a great hotel here. Are you just staying here on holiday?'

'No, I live here, too. My fiancé has his own business. He runs a fleet of fishing boats for tourists, a fishing club and a visitors' centre.'

'He must do very well for himself,' Tom said.

'Nothing but the best for my sister,' Vince said. 'You've got expensive tastes, haven't you, Cameo? Tom, shall we get some more drinks?'

Tom agreed and the two men stood up. Cameo pushed her seat back to allow Tom to pass and as she leaned forward, Ellie was suddenly taken by a gold locket hanging around her neck. It caught the light and winked brightly at her. It was oval-shaped and engraved on the edge of it was a mermaid with a diamond-encrusted tail. It was very unusual but Ellie had seen it before. She suddenly felt very dizzy and a cold waft of ice ran down her back, making her shiver involuntarily.

'Are you all right?' Cameo said. 'You've gone as white as a sheet. You look as though you've seen a ghost.'

Ellie concentrated really hard to recover herself.

'I'm fine, really. Just a bit of

sun-stroke, I think. I came over a bit dizzy.'

'You should drink some water,' Cameo said knowledgeably, 'and not too much alcohol. I'll go and get you some.'

'Thank you,' Ellie said. 'I think you're right.'

Cameo went to join Vince and Tom at the bar, and Ellie saw Tom look over at her, concerned. She waved at him to stop him fussing. Then she looked at Cameo again. Where on earth had she got that locket? There couldn't be two like it, surely.

She was waiting for the others to come back and looked around idly. Then the second shock came and sent a further tremor through Ellie's body. Harrison was walking towards the bar with a dark-haired girl beside him. She was olive-skinned, small, petite and very beautiful and she had her arm linked through Harrison's. He had spotted Vince, Cameo and Tom at the bar and joined them. Ellie watched them as they all introduced each other and then Tom pointed in her direction and Harrison lifted his arm in a greeting.

Oh, no, she thought, that's all I need. She was still feeling unwell and suddenly they were all coming towards her with trays of drinks and she wished she was in her chalet — alone. Vince pulled some more chairs around the small table in front of Ellie and as they made themselves comfortable, Harrison introduced Ellie to the young Kenyan girl with him.

'This is Kim Wakahki, a researcher from Nairobi. She's helping out at the animal centre a few days a week. Kim, this is Ellie Britten, a friend of the family.'

Ellie winced at that description of their relationship and managed to change it into a smile as Kim held out a slim, brown hand.

'Pleased to meet you, Ellie. I hear you're not feeling too well. Too much sun today?'

Ellie took the glass of water that Tom was handing her.

'Oh, it's nothing. I'm sure I'll be fine in a moment.'

'It can be a disaster if you're not used to it,' Cameo said.

'Yes, we can't have you ill on your second day,' Harrison added.

Ellie sipped the water.

'I'll be fine,' she insisted. 'Please, don't fuss.'

'Harrison has told me all about you,' Kim said, sensing that Ellie wanted to change the subject. 'I think he is like a big brother to you, no?'

Ellie wondered what he had told her but just smiled again and said, 'Oh, yes, just like a big brother.'

Cameo put her drink down.

'Come on, let's dance,' she said.

Kim agreed, but Ellie wanted some air and Harrison wanted some food, so they all stood and disappeared in different directions. Tom followed the two girls on to the dance floor and Harrison and Vince went to get themselves some food.

'I'll just go for a walk and clear my head,' Ellie told them all.

She stepped down off the lounge decking area and walked along beside the pool. There were underwater lights shining through the water, casting a strange green glow around the terrace. Soon she had left the vicinity of the hotel's main buildings and was wandering through the gardens towards the steps that led down to the beach.

She could hear the muted sounds of the group singing and a soft murmur of voices that melted together behind her. She followed the steps that wound down to the sandy shoreline of the creek. It was a private area just for the hotel and no-one was down there.

The beach bar closed at eight o'clock. The frames of sunbeds remained on the sands, the mattresses all collected up and stored in a little hut next to the shower rooms.

Ellie went and sat on a low wall beside the bar and watched the tide rolling up and down, gently sucking at the sand. The area was swarming with little crabs scuttling in and out of their sand holes, making Ellie keep her feet well back.

She had been sitting there for a good fifteen minutes when she heard footsteps advancing towards her. She made no attempt to move or look round to see who was there. She knew already.

'There you are,' Harrison said. 'I thought you might be down here.'

'It's so beautiful,' Ellie replied. 'So tranquil. I still can't believe I'm really here.'

Harrison sat on the wall next to her.

'How are you feeling? All right now?'

Ellie nodded.

'You really must be careful about drinking enough water while you're out here,' Harrison warned her. 'You could get really ill if you get dehydrated.'

She almost felt like laughing at his concern for her. He hadn't shown the least interest in her for ten years, so it hardly seemed appropriate to suddenly feign all this anxiety.

'You don't need to worry, Harrison,' she assured him. 'I am drinking enough, honest. It wasn't lack of water that made me feel faint. Something else . . . it doesn't matter.'

'What do you mean, something else? Cameo said you looked like you'd seen a ghost. What has upset you?'

'I don't really want to talk about it.'

'I don't understand,' Harrison persisted. 'What is it? Maybe I can help.'

'Really, it's nothing I want to discuss.'

She got up and started walking, following the shoreline towards the mouth of the creek where it opened up into the Indian Ocean. Her heart was pounding and she wanted to confide in Harrison. It had been so easy before, when they had been together. But that was back then. This was now and everything was different.

They walked in silence for a short way. Ellie felt like crying, but that might have been because she was thinking about her parents, and how she had lost them for ever, not far from this very spot.

'I'm sorry about your parents,' Harrison ventured, almost as though he had read her thoughts.

Ellie stopped and turned to him.

'Are you?' she asked sharply. 'Are you really? It happened five years ago, Harrison. You haven't spoken to me for ten years! If I hadn't come out here with Tom you wouldn't be speaking to me now, would you?'

'Ouch, that hurts,' he said in a feeble attempt at joviality.

Sticking his hands in his pockets he pushed some sand around with the toe of his deck shoes.

'But it's true.'

'I'm sorry. I'm no good. Happy now?'

Ellie sighed and started walking again.

'It doesn't matter to you whether I'm happy or not, so why don't you just go back to Kim and the party and leave me alone?'

'I can't. You've got me curious now. What made you take off suddenly? Is it that you're jealous of Kim?' Harrison said. 'Is that why you suddenly feigned sickness and disappeared all melodramatic?'

'That had nothing to do with Kim. I really don't care who you are with. I told you, it was something else and I don't want to talk about it.'

'Look,' Harrison persisted, 'what we had was really good, but it was getting too serious. You were only eighteen and I was approaching thirty. I was your first love. It wouldn't have been right. You should have been out with all your friends, playing the field, having your pick of all the boys, not settling down with me.'

Ellie rounded on him again.

'What makes you think I wanted to settle down with you? I was just out for a good time. You had a fast car and I was showing off to my friends.'

'You were falling in love with me,' Harrison said.

'Oh, you are so conceited. How did we get on to this subject anyway?'

'Your jealousy when you saw me come in with Kim.'

The conversation was not going well.

'Harrison, can we just leave this where it is? The real reason I had to get out and get some fresh air was Cameo is wearing my mother's locket.'

3

There was a heavy silence, broken only by the sound of lapping water, as Harrison considered what she'd said.

'OK? Happy now you've dragged that out of me?'

'What do you mean, Ellie? How can Cameo be wearing your mother's locket?' Harrison asked.

'I don't know,' Ellie said, suddenly wishing she hadn't confided in him. 'That's the whole point. How can she be? My father had it specially made for my mother and she wore it all the time. She never took it off, but when their bodies were found, the locket was missing. It was quite valuable, so it was assumed that whoever had . . . '

She struggled to continue.

'Whoever murdered them had stolen their yacht and their jewellery,' she managed to say.

Tears welled up in her eyes and spilled over, rolling down her cheeks. Harrison saw her wipe them away with the back of her hand, trying to disguise the fact that she was crying.

'Hey, come on, no tears,' he said, realising that he was 'way off the mark with the reason Ellie had wanted to be alone.

Unsure what to do, he put his arm around her shoulder and soothed her by saying, 'It could just be a similar locket and you're mistaken.'

Ellie shook her head vehemently.

'Definitely not. I would recognise it anywhere. It is my mother's. Seeing it has brought all the memories back again. I don't know what to do. How on earth did Cameo get hold of it?'

Harrison couldn't answer the question. He still thought that she'd made a mistake.

'Look, you've had a few drinks, and you're probably feeling quite emotional being out here in Kenya for the first time, back where the tragedy took place. You've been thinking about your parents and about what happened, reliving it all. You're bound to be a bit sensitive.'

'What are you saying, that you don't believe me? I'm not making this up, you know. I'll bet money on the fact that the engraving inside the locket says, **All my love R**. It stands for Roger, my father. Now just leave me alone, will you? I don't know why you followed me down here in the first place. I expect Kim will be looking for you.'

She stormed off down the beach back towards the hotel, still sobbing. Harrison leaped after her and grabbed her by the arm.

'I didn't say I didn't believe you, I'm just trying to find a rational explanation.'

'Oh, so I'm not being rational now!' Ellie screeched. 'Let go of my arm.'

'Stop screeching.'

She slapped him, quite irrationally, in her distress, and as he let go of her arm to touch his smarting cheek she attempted a fast walk across the sand but was impeded by her mules and ended up tripping over. Before she could regain her poise, Harrison was pulling her to her feet and picking her mules up off the sand.

'Ellie, stop getting hysterical and listen to me,' Harrison begged her.

'Oh, so I've gone from irrational to hyst . . .'

Ellie stopped, suddenly aware that Harrison was right up close to her face and as his lips touched hers she felt a sudden spark of energy flash through her whole body. He kissed her gently and tentatively, as though gauging her response before throwing himself into a passionate embrace. The warm night air wound her flimsy dress around her legs and blew her hair against her face as Harrison drew her in closer against his body and caressed her hair as he deepened his kiss so that she almost lost her breath and started to melt against him as her knees threatened to give way.

Suddenly she realised what was happening.

Oh, no, not again. Don't do this to me, she thought, wanting to pull away but feeling drawn to him like a magnet.

The ten years since they had last been together like this shrank to no time at all. After a kiss that seemed to last an eternity, she came to her senses and forced herself back to the present. Tears were welling up inside her again, and she just wanted to be alone, with her thoughts and feelings.

She looked up at Harrison and very quietly formed the words, 'Just leave me alone, please. I don't want this.'

She walked away from him back up the slope towards the comforting sounds of the hotel and the safety of crowds. As she walked through the lounge she saw the others, still drinking and laughing together. Kim seemed to be enjoying herself and not unduly worried as to Harrison's whereabouts. Were they an item, she wondered. Did it matter to her? She wasn't sure.

Harrison had unlocked feelings she had thought were banished long ago. She should be cross that he thought he could give her such a weak explanation of his actions a decade ago, and then kiss her and confuse her all over again. She should forget what had happened tonight and not allow it to go any further. Another holiday romance with Harrison Grey was not on her agenda.

'Are you OK now?' Tom asked as she sat back down with the others.

'I'm fine, really. It was just a touch of sunstroke. I promise I'll drink more water.'

'You're not as white as a sheet any more,' he commented. 'In fact you look very flushed.'

'Where's Harrison, I wonder,' Kim said just as he walked into view coming from the same direction as Ellie.

Tom looked at Ellie's flushed face again and a slight frown furrowed his brow forming an unspoken question as he began putting two and two together. Ellie looked away quickly.

'These singers are very good,' she said to Cameo, trying not to stare at the locket round her neck. 'Are they regulars here?'

'Yes. They do three nights a week here and three at the Hotel Simbani.'

Ellie looked for something else to ask her, unable to look either at Tom or Kim as Harrison joined them.

'Anyone ready for another drink?' Harrison asked.

'Where have you been?' Kim questioned him.

Ellie didn't catch the reply as she asked Cameo, 'Where's your fiancé tonight, working?'

'Ryder? Yes, he's at his fishing club. It does get a bit tedious for me sometimes, but then that's big business for you. He's going to be a multimillionaire by the time he's forty and then we'll retire and really live the jetset life.'

'It's all right for some,' Ellie replied, knowing that her mother's locket was quite valuable and should by rights be with her.

The band had quietened down and were now singing romantic ballads. Vince and Kim got up to dance together and Harrison asked Cameo to join him. Tom shrugged his shoulders at Ellie.

'Looks like you've got me,' he said.

Ellie smiled and replied, 'Come on then.'

The next morning, at the breakfast table, Vince joined Ellie and Tom.

'I hear you're off to the Kipepeo Butterfly Farm today with Kim,' he said to them. 'I came to remind you to visit the Gedi ruins while you are there. It's just nearby.'

Ellie shook her head.

'Tom's going, but I'm staying here to do a bit of sunbathing and reading.'

Tom drained the tea from his cup.

'I'll ask Kim if we can visit them,' he said. 'I hear they are very beautiful.'

'Yes, that is true,' Vince told them, 'but in a haunting and eerie way.'

'I'll take plenty of film with me.'

'It will be difficult to capture such a

strange place on film,' Vince told him. 'Gedi has a sinister reputation, you know. Local people have always been apprehensive about it. There are many ghost stories and tales of strange happenings.'

Ellie shivered despite the heat.

'I'm glad I'm not going,' she said. 'I hate spooks.'

'Archaeologists working on the site have said that they experienced the feeling that they were being watched from behind walls. You'll see what I mean when you get there, Tom,' Vince continued. 'The place makes your spine tingle very easily.'

Kim arrived then and they rose from the table.

'Good morning, everyone,' she said brightly. 'Are you ready, Tom?'

Tom picked up his two bags of camera equipment.

'Yep. Vince has just been telling me all about the Gedi ruins.'

'We can go if you want to,' Kim said. 'It's a very interesting place.'

'So I understand,' Tom replied as they departed, leaving Vince and Ellie at the entrance to the dining area.

'Well,' Vince said, 'I'll leave you to your sunbathing. This afternoon, if you would like to, I can take you out on the boat. I've arranged some flowers, you know, for you to scatter at sea.'

'Oh, thank you, Vince. That's very kind of you. I hope I'm not putting you to any trouble.'

Vince put up his hand.

'No trouble at all. I'll see you later then.'

Ellie went back to her chalet. The maid service was cleaning the room, so she just grabbed her sun-bag and towel and made her way to the pool area. Finding a sun lounger in just the right spot she made herself comfortable for a relaxing tanning session.

By the time it was one o'clock, Ellie had turned herself over several times, moved in and out of the shade and applied copious amounts of lotion. Now she was lying on her stomach, resting on her elbows reading a book when someone cast a shadow across the pages. She looked up to see who was getting between her and the sun. She squinted behind her sunglasses and found herself staring up at Harrison.

'Hello,' he said. 'All on your own?'

'Yes. Kim has taken Tom to the butterfly farm. Shouldn't you be at the animal centre, injecting a baby elephant, or measuring a giraffe?'

Harrison laughed.

'I've got special dispensation. I told Dad I wanted to come and see you. He seemed very pleased.'

'I hope he doesn't get too excited by it. What do you want?'

'That's not much of a greeting.'

'It's the best I can do.'

'I'm sorry about last night. Blame it on the drink.'

'Oh, thanks a lot,' Ellie replied. 'So you have to be under the influence of alcohol to be able to kiss me now.'

'That's not what I meant.' Harrison sighed. 'I'm not very good with words.'

'I know that already. Is that why you went off ten years ago and never spoke to me again?'

'I'm not good at goodbyes. I suppose I felt it was best at the time . . . you know . . . make a clean break.'

'You took the cowards' way out and broke my heart.'

Ellie sat up and pulled a T-shirt over her bikini, then reached for the bottle of mineral water under the sun lounger.

'I see you're drinking plenty,' he commented.

'Don't change the subject. How could you do what you did to me, just disappear without a trace? I still can't believe you did it. You know I kept telling myself that there would be a good reason for your silence, that you were going to come back. Then my dad got a letter from Ernest and he said you'd gone to Thailand with your new girlfriend! How cruel is that?'

'I'm sorry. I don't know what else to say. You're right, it was cruel. I didn't deserve you, but you were just too young. You hadn't known anyone else. Things could have been different if you had been a bit older.'

Ellie could feel her heart starting to race. What was Harrison trying to say, that he still wanted her? Did he want them to start again, after all this time? Was he trying to say that? Was that what the kiss was all about? Maybe he did want to start up a relationship again, but after her little outburst last night on the beach, he would think she wasn't interested and he wouldn't want to risk rejection.

Before she had a chance to say anything else, Tom and Kim arrived back, full of greetings and enthusing about the butterflies and the ruins at Gedi.

'You should have come, Ellie,' Tom said. 'You'd have loved it.'

'Yes, maybe I should have,' she replied.

Harrison detected a churlish tone in her voice but the others didn't. She started to put her things away in her bag.

'What brings you over here this morning?' Tom asked Harrison, trying to sound innocent.

'Come on, I expect you are starving,' Ellie butted in. 'Let's have some lunch. Vince is taking us out on the boat this afternoon. We mustn't be late.'

Harrison smiled.

'Well, actually, I came to tell you that I've a place for you both on my mini-safari tomorrow. It's to the Tsavo National Park, staying overnight at the tented Moja campsite.'

Ellie stopped in her tracks.

'Tents, in the middle of a wild-life reserve? Are you quite mad?'

'It's a purpose-built camp. You'll be quite safe, I promise.'

'Great!' Tom said excitedly.

Ellie was ignored, as Harrison and Tom discussed the safari details. Kim leaned forward and touched Ellie on her arm.

'You'll love it,' she said. 'You will.'

It was cooler out at sea. Vince took the helm of Blue Sprite and guided her out of the creek into the open blue waters of the Indian Ocean. Across the estuary there were reefs and the waves danced about quite choppily. Ellie was a little green around the gills, but after they had reached more open sea it became calmer although the waves were quite high.

'You're not in the Med now,' Vince said, seeing her discomfort.

He threw her a packet of pills.

'Take a few of those. You'll be fine.'

Ellie punched a few tablets out of the card and swallowed them with yet more water from the bottle she carried everywhere with her now. Feeling slightly seasick was nothing compared to how her parents must have felt when they knew they were not going to survive after the thieves stormed their boat. She stared wistfully out to sea and tried to imagine where they had been sailing when it had happened.

They hadn't gone far when Vince cut the engine and it was eerily silent, just the lapping of the sea against the hull which brought memories flooding back to Ellie of trips on her parents' yacht. Vince seemed quite knowledgeable on the subject of what happened to them that fateful day, which surprised Ellie.

'They can't have been too far out at sea,' he explained, 'because their bodies were washed up on the shore. They were heading for the marina at Basanga so my guess is that it probably happened around here.'

Tom put his arm around Ellie's shoulder and gave it a squeeze, while Vince went inside the cabin and brought out a lovely wreath of exotic flowers. He handed them to Ellie.

'Take your time, Ellie,' he said kindly. She stood on the stern and bowed her head as she mouthed a silent prayer. Tom and Vince stood behind her with their hands clasped in reverence. Then Ellie hurled the wreath into the sea and watched it bobbing up and down with the swell.

'I love you both,' she whispered.

They waited for a few minutes, Tom unsure whether or not to say a few words and Vince not wanting to start the engine again too soon, but Ellie herself pulled her shoulders up.

'Thank you very much. I'd like to go back now,' she said.

When they arrived back at the marina, Cameo was watching from the wooden quay. She took the mooring rope as Tom threw the coil at her and tied them up alongside.

'Are you all right?' Cameo asked Ellie, as she offered her hand to help her down on to dry land. 'Were the flowers OK?'

'Did you organise them?' Ellie asked.

Cameo nodded.

'Women are usually better at that kind of thing than men.'

'They were lovely, just right. Will you come and have a drink with us?'

'Can't.'

She indicated a man standing over by the fuel pumps.

'Ryder's got plans. I have to go in a minute. Thanks, though. I'll see you later.'

As she walked away, Ellie watched as Cameo caught up with her fiancé and gave him a kiss. He seemed familiar to Ellie.

'What's Ryder's surname, Vince?' she asked as he locked the cabin door.

'Leason,' he told her. 'Ryder Leason. Why? Do you know him?'

'He does seem familiar, but I don't recognise the name. I must be mistaken.'

But she was sure she had seen him before, not recently though. But where? She racked her brains, not recalling where it was she had seen him, but instinctively sensing that he was not good news.

4

Ellie's dreams that night were complicated and intricate, involving one-legged pirates with coloured wooden parrots on their shoulders, Harrison kissing her and Ryder Leason pursuing her along a beach where she was cut off from the tide.

She woke with her heart thumping wildly. Who was this Ryder Leason? If only she could remember where she'd seen him before. She glanced at her travel alarm clock and saw that it was only half past five. Six minutes to go before it was set to go off. It took her a few moments to bring herself back to the present and remember why it was that she needed to get up so early.

A glance at her overnight bag packed and waiting by the door reminded her of the safari trip today. She switched on the bedside lamp and slipped out from beneath the crumpled sheet. She walked over to the dressing-table, the floor cool and pleasant on the soles of her feet, and flipping the lid off the small kettle on the tea-making tray she filled it carefully from a bottle of water and switched it on to boil. She waited until she heard the faint hiss of the element before going into the bath-room.

She stepped under the shower. The lukewarm water bubbled and fizzed on her skin. She closed her eyes and let the water cascade over her head. Her thoughts, now more coherent as the strange dream receded, returned to the question of Harrison and the feelings for him that had resurfaced against her wishes.

She scolded herself. Having not seen or heard from him in ten years, here she was, barely off the plane, and already she had allowed him to kiss her. After vowing never to get involved with him again, he was creeping under her skin, hijacking her dreams and she couldn't stop him.

Ellie rubbed her skin vigorously with her body scrub, as though trying to erase the man from under her skin. He'd left her broken hearted and subconsciously she was still holding a place in her heart for him. She rinsed the soap off her body and, switching off the taps, she stepped out and towelled herself dry.

So what was she going to do? Did she still want him? And where did Kim fit into all this? She appeared to be very friendly with Harrison. As Ellie got herself dressed for the safari, she thought back to the day before at the pool-side when she and Harrison had been interrupted by Tom and Kim returning from the butterfly farm.

She recalled Harrison hinting at the fact that things could have been so different if she had been older, well, she was older now. Did he still want her, or just a holiday romance? She asked herself all these questions and could not find any answers.

It had all happened so quickly, and if she analysed just what it was that had happened, it all boiled down to an unexpected meeting, a few hints and a stolen kiss on the beach. If she hadn't come here with Tom, would Harrison ever have tried to contact her? Probably not, which led her to believe that he was just an opportunist, out for what he could get.

Ellie drank a mug of coffee while contemplating the idea of Harrison as a cold-hearted, cunning gigolo.

She was just tying her safari boots when a gentle tap came on the door.

'Ellie,' Tom called softly

She opened the door to see him ready with his rucksack and familiar camera bag over his shoulder, his eyes still heavy with sleep. He looked like a little boy on Christmas morning. She suddenly felt a pang of guilt. They had made such plans together for their image library, **Nesbitt and Britten Images**, and she had barely mentioned it or shown interest since they'd arrived here and Harrison had burst back on to the scene.

Ellie decided then and there that she and Harrison were just not going to work. She was going to ignore any advances from him on this safari trip today and pay more attention to Tom. She'd shown Harrison that he couldn't just muscle in on her friendship with Tom or expect her to drop everything and alter her plans. There were other people to consider.

'Ready then?' Tom asked.

She nodded and smiled at him.

'Absolutely, I can't wait.'

She picked up her pack and they walked quickly through the near deserted hotel, as the sounds of the dawn echoed around them. The air held the promise of another hot day. The mini bus was just pulling up outside as Ellie and Tom reached the front porch.

'At least they didn't forget us,' Tom declared as Conrad, who had brought them home from the animal centre before, climbed out of the driver's side, opened the sliding-door to let them in, then packed their bags in the rear.

''Morning,' a wide-awake Harrison said from the front passenger seat.

Ellie and Tom murmured a greeting in reply and climbed into the two remaining seats inside. The other seats were taken up by a mousey-looking man with his wife and their two teenage children, and another couple. They all introduced themselves as Conrad took the wheel and drove slowly down the hotel drive. Outside on the main road, they joined up with another mini bus of tourists and the small convoy headed off.

Tom made small talk with their companions and Ellie punctuated his sentences with the odd smile or agreement. They were obviously thought to be a couple. Ellie did not correct them or try to explain their relationship. She hoped Harrison was listening, although due to the age of the mini bus and the roughness of the road, noise kept conversation to a minimum, and any exchange with Harrison in the front was impossible.

Ellie was grateful and sat back to enjoy the view. It was a two-hour drive to Mombasa. She recognised it from when they had first arrived in Kenya. It was a jumbled labyrinth of narrow streets with carved, overhanging balconies and elaborate wooden doors, which were highly ornamental and decorated traditionally with large brass studs.

They left the hustle and bustle behind and were soon driving north out of the town and heading towards Tsavo East National Park. After a breakfast stop and a look around a souvenir shop, just before ten o'clock, Conrad turned off the bumpy main road on to an even bumpier track and there in front of them was the simple entrance to one of the most well-known nature reserves in Kenya.

They pulled into a parking area before actually entering the park and they all stretched their legs and had a drink. Conrad opened up the roof of the camper bus so that they could stand up if they wanted as they were driving through the reserve and get a better view of the animals.

'Will we get to see much?' Ellie asked.

Harrison seized the opportunity to speak to her.

'Yes. Conrad has been on the radio to the convoy ahead of us and they are reporting back to him right now with sightings.'

Ellie felt a little shiver of anticipation. Harrison went over to talk to the security guards on the gate and Ellie found herself watching him. The hot climate suited him. He was tanned and more muscular than before. She had to blink and look away as she started to relive the kiss on the beach. She turned and caught Tom's eyes on her. She wandered over to him and he held a bottle of water out to her.

'Drink?'

She nodded and took the bottle from

him. There was an inkling of an atmosphere between them. He'd been watching her and thinking, what?

'Harrison followed you down to the beach the other night, didn't he?' Tom stated.

Ellie stopped drinking and nodded.

'He came to see if I was all right, you know, after I felt dizzy.'

Tom sighed.

'When you two split up before, who dumped whom?'

Ellie prickled at Tom's direct question.

'No-one dumped anyone. We just stopped seeing each other.'

'There must have been a reason,' Tom persisted.

Ellie did not want to have this conversation so she tipped the bottle up and started drinking from it again.

'Look,' Tom said casually, 'I'm concerned, that's all. I don't want to see you getting hurt.'

Ellie was visibly bristling as she handed the water bottle back to Tom.

'Thanks,' she said from between pursed lips.

'You looked a bit flushed when you came back. Did he kiss you?' Tom asked softly.

'Yes,' Ellie threw at him. 'Yes, he did, and thank you for your concern, but I am perfectly able to look after myself. I'm not getting involved, but if I did, I really don't see the need for you to concern yourself.'

The expression on Tom's face was one of suppressed misery and it was at that point that Ellie suddenly realised that Tom's feelings for her were more than just friendly. Her immediate reaction was surprise.

She couldn't deny they were good friends, and worked really well together, but nothing more had ever crossed her mind before, especially as they had already been working together at the magazine for several years with no hint of romantic involvement. But now, as she thought back over the past few months, she realised that the signs had been there all along. She had chosen not to read them.

Tom saw the sudden awareness in her eyes and felt embarrassed and awkward.

'Oh, Tom,' she said, 'you . . . I'm sorry. I never realised . . . '

He held up his hand.

'Don't say anything. Why should you have realised how I felt? They were my feelings, and obviously not yours, too. I just wish I had known about Harrison before we came out here. I feel a bit of a fool.'

'Don't be. There wasn't anything to know. We were history. I had no idea he was out here, truly. I can't deny we had something once but it was all a long time ago. I don't think we can go back to how it was before.'

'Are you sure about that?' Tom asked quietly. 'I've seen the way you look at him.'

Ellie was lost for words, but she was painfully aware that she and Tom definitely would not be able to go back to how they were before, not now Tom had admitted his feelings for her.

Conrad was calling everyone back into the bus so Ellie shrugged her shoulders in reply and climbed back in, glad that their conversation had been interrupted. She busied herself getting her binoculars out of her bag.

The bus lurched through the entrance, following in the wake of the other bus in their convoy. They had barely got into the reserve before they all ground to a halt where a cheetah was gazing at them from the bush, just yards from the buses. Ellie's eyes roamed from the animal's sleek back to the back of Harrison's neck, and wondered how she was going to manage two days trying to ignore him when he was in such close proximity.

The game-filled savannah stretched for miles in every direction. The bus jerked on and bumped along the tracks, its passengers looking in wonder as they passed herds of zebra and small families of giraffes. Conrad braked suddenly behind the second bus.

'Ah, tembo, tembo,' he said pointing over to the left.

'Elephants,' Harrison translated.

He'd managed to position himself standing right next to Ellie. She was concentrating hard on looking through her binoculars at the herd of elephants in the distance, trying to focus on them and on the baby elephants being protected in the middle of the group.

She wasn't really aware of Harrison so close to her until he slipped his arm around her shoulders and brought his cheek up close to hers pointing and directing her gaze.

'Oh, my goodness,' she exclaimed. 'It's just brilliant.'

Tom tried to keep a neutral countenance, but it was difficult when Ellie's voice sounded so silky and she could have been talking about the proximity of Harrison rather than the wonderful vista of animals viewed in their natural surroundings.

They stopped for lunch at a rest site

with a small shop-cum-cafeteria. The parties from both buses followed Harrison and Conrad up over a small bank and looked down at a large, muddy water-hole where they pointed out some hippos in the distance, wallowing at the edges of the water on the far side of the hole with just their heads poking out of the water and the only sign of movement, a twitching ear now and again or a small bird swooping down to peck insects from their hides.

Hundreds of large birds had also congregated safely opposite the hippos, looking like a mass of black cloud.

'I can't believe people camp here,' Ellie said, as Conrad pointed out lion tracks on the dusty ground. 'Don't they get attacked? I read that two lions stalked and killed workers who were building the railway link between Lake Victoria and the coast back at the turn of the century.'

Conrad laughed.

'You read too much. As long as you obey the law of the land and respect the animals, you won't go far wrong. They don't want to attack and eat you. Come we must be off now. Plenty more animals to see.'

★ ★ ★

The camp-fire hissed and crackled. Apart from a few lanterns dotted around the clearing this was all the light there was and the faces of the intrepid tour party sat round it expectantly were strangely illuminated. Behind the fire, beyond the primitive log fence, the ground sloped away down to the river and in the flickering light Ellie could just make out the silhouette of a lone elephant, and the rustling of loose bushes and twigs beneath his feet as he lumbered slowly alongside the camp site.

It was amazing enough that they were this close to nature but Conrad had told them that sometimes the elephants actually walked right through the campsite!

The safari party guests were all drinking happily together as the camp host, Samuel, entertained them all with stories of the bush and jokes which had a surprising Western humour about them. Tom was chatting to their fellow mini-bus companions. It appeared he was ignoring Ellie.

Well, she could hardly blame him. If that's how he wanted to deal with this bizarre and embarrassing situation, that was fine by her. She had enough on her plate to contemplate.

Since they had arrived here, Harrison had not been seen. They had all been shown to their tents and then later picked up and escorted back down to the main tent for dinner and evening entertainment.

Where was he, she wondered, as she drained the glass of her second gin and tonic and stared at the flames. Soon, it was time to retire. She stood up, made her excuses and started up the slope towards the main tent.

'Make sure you have a guide escort

you to your tent,' Samuel called out to her.

She put her hand up without looking back round at the gathering she had left.

'I will,' she shouted back to him.

Tom hadn't even acknowledged her leaving.

In the main tent, the guides were enjoying a few beers and a game of cards. Harrison had joined them, and at the mere sight of him Ellie's pulse started to race just that bit faster and a warm wave of emotion rushed over her in an instant. She found him impossible to ignore.

'Would someone escort me to my tent?' she asked, struggling to keep her voice steady and not look directly at Harrison.

She tried to ignore the little voice inside her head pleading for Harrison to offer. The unspoken prayer was answered.

'Sure,' he said, standing up.

The guides were happy not to have to

interrupt their game of cards and were quite oblivious to the current of feelings that was assaulting Ellie from every direction. They walked together away from all the partying, up the path towards the dark shapes of the guest tents.

It was strangely quiet and neither of them felt the need to speak. Every now and then an unfamiliar noise would invade the still, evening air. Ellie was trembling, but somehow she didn't think it was from fear of being out here at night in the middle of a game reserve. A sudden screech from very nearby pushed Ellie into boldly linking her arm into Harrison's.

'What was that?' she asked, nervously.

Harrison laughed.

'Only some bird. We probably frightened it.'

'This is the first time I've ever been anywhere like this,' she defended herself. 'It's quite scary, but I'm excited, too.'

'I can feel that,' Harrison told her. 'You're trembling.'

His voice was thick with innuendo. The perfectly innocent words tumbled from his lips, cloaked in hidden meaning. By the time they reached Ellie's tent, she was practically shaking with desire and need for him. How could she have thought she would be able to suppress such longing? Did he feel the same? They stopped a few feet from the wooden decking outside her sleeping quarters and the atmosphere between them was electric.

'I hope you sleep all right,' Harrison said. 'Remember, if you get spooked, don't come running out into the night, straight into the path of a marauding elephant.'

Ellie shivered. She suddenly panicked that he was going to leave her there and walk back to continue his drinking with the guides. Was he teasing her? She wasn't sure what to do but she knew that she couldn't let him go. Here was the perfect moment for him to take her into his arms, but he turned and walked away. The tension continued to hang around them. He must have felt it, too, but there wasn't even the hint of a good-night kiss from him.

'Harrison?' she called after him, trying not to sound like a desperate woman.

He stopped and turned round slowly. Was there a glint of a tantalising smile on his lips, a hidden agenda behind those blue eyes that seemed to penetrate right through her?

She felt a stirring somewhere deep inside her.

'Sorry,' she forced the words out as carefully as possible. 'Could you just check there aren't any snakes or anything inside?'

He made to look back towards the main tent and the distant murmur of voices, as though trying to decide if he could spare the time to carry out tent inspection while his beer was getting warm! Ellie wondered suddenly if she was going to regret this and end up making a complete fool of herself, but Harrison had started to walk back towards her.

5

Harrison unzipped the heavy canvas tent and stepped inside, holding the flap up to let Ellie in. She stood behind him, waiting for him to check for snakes. Then she became aware that the lantern on the small table was lit. She was sure she had switched it off before she had left the tent earlier and Harrison hadn't had time to light it. He was busy looking under the camp-bed for snakes and shining his torch around into the corners.

'There, all clear,' he assured her, standing up. 'You're safe now.'

Her eyes swept around to confirm that she was indeed safe and came to rest on a bottle of champagne in an ice-bucket and two glasses on another little table towards the back of the tent. Realisation dawned on her.

'You've already been in here tonight,

while I was down with the others. You brought this champagne in here, all ready for your grand seduction scene, is it? Oh, I'm so stupid, and you're so sure of yourself. How dare you assume that I . . . '

Harrison took hold of her and brought his lips down on hers to silence her rage. Was she that easy, she asked herself and finally managed to push him away.

'What's the matter?' he asked.

Ellie breathed deeply and tried to steady herself. What was the matter? This was what she wanted, wasn't it? But she was thinking again of how he had abandoned her before and she was furious at how presumptuous he had been tonight.

'How dare you think you can come in here when I'm not here and plan all this out just as you want! I'm worth more than that, so you can just forget it. Please go and leave me alone.'

She pushed him towards the tent opening.

'Hey,' Harrison said indignantly, 'don't forget, you dragged me in here. You want me just as much as I want you. Come on, Ellie, admit it, and I'll admit I was a fool to ever let you go. It was complicated, but I can make amends. Let me show you how I feel. Give us another chance.'

'Complicated!'

Ellie moved towards him and put her arms up to push him away.

'Cowardly, more like.'

Harrison stood firm and caught hold of her wrists. Then gently, but firmly, he pulled her towards him and bent down to kiss her neck. As he felt her weaken and begin to relax against him he released her wrists and pulled her nearer to him. She gave a little shiver. Her arms hung loosely at her side and she inhaled sharply as he brought his lips down on hers and kissed her again.

Later, Harrison released Ellie from his embrace, and proceeded to uncork the champagne. He poured two glasses and handed one to Ellie. She took the glass as Harrison sat on the edge of the bed to drink his, and signalled for her to join him.

'I'm sorry I came in here earlier. I can't deny that I had hoped to win you back, but please believe me when I say that I was waiting for a move from you first. I needed to know that you still really wanted me, too. If you hadn't asked me to search your tent for uninvited guests I'd have just kept walking.'

'You mean you wouldn't have tried anything all? You'd have just walked away and given up on me so easily?'

Harrison grinned at her.

'Well, I might have had another tactic, but you'll never know, now.'

Ellie wanted to ask him what had been complicated ten years ago that he just upped and left. What is there now for us? But she was afraid to spoil the moment, afraid to voice her doubts. She had to face reality. He lived and worked in Kenya and she was a successful magazine editor on the brink of a new business venture in which she had already invested money.

She couldn't possibly give it all up to move out here, could she? She certainly couldn't see Harrison giving up this lifestyle. Maybe they had been doomed anyway all along and now all she had done was set herself to be hurt all over again.

'Penny for them,' Harrison said, frowning and dropping his head to one side. 'You look so serious all of a sudden.'

Ellie forced a smile.

'I was just thinking of my parents,' she lied. 'They would have enjoyed this safari. It's a shame they didn't reach Kenyan soil alive to see it all.'

'You miss them a lot, don't you?'

Ellie nodded. She gulped down the champagne and let Harrison refill her glass.

'Why on earth didn't they come here on a package holiday? What made them decide to sail around the world rather than go overland? I know your dad was into sailing in a big way, but that was a tremendous thing to decide to do at their age.'

Ellie's parents had spent years together building up their business and Ellie hadn't come along until they were both in their late thirties.

'I don't know what made them do it, really. I know the business wasn't doing very well. I think Dad just got a good offer from another company to buy him out, and he just thought, let's do it.'

'Why wasn't the business doing well?' Harrison frowned. 'I always thought it was very stable.'

'It was for a long time, but after that awful business when Dad got ripped off for over five hundred thousand pounds, it never really . . .'

She stopped mid-sentence.

'Never really what?' Harrison asked her. 'What's the matter?'

'Max Hooper!' Ellie exclaimed out of the blue.

'Max who? What are you on about?'

'Twelve years ago, oh, you remember,

don't you? Max Hooper was Dad's whiz-kid accountant. He embezzled the money and disappeared. He was never caught.'

Harrison was still frowning.

'I remember vaguely, but I'm not sure I see what you're getting at.'

'Cameo's fiancé. I thought I had seen Ryder Leason somewhere before.'

'Go on.'

'Well, I know I was only young and I didn't see him very often, and he has changed, but . . . '

'Are you saying what I think you are?' Harrison said incredulously.

Ellie's eyes were wide.

'I think Ryder Leason is Max Hooper.'

Harrison was shaking his head in disbelief.

'You can't be serious! I know he's loaded, but I've known him for a couple of years now. He seems an OK sort of a bloke. I can't believe he's an embezzler. He's given loads to different charities out here, even sponsors a local school.'

'Maybe he's got a guilty conscience. Besides, have you ever met an embezzler? Would you recognise one?' Ellie asked him.

'Well, no,' Harrison admitted.

'Con-men are usually very cool, calculating, clever people. The more I think about it, the more I think he is. I know Max Hooper had longish hair and a droopy moustache but, oh, I don't know . . . Ryder . . . there's something familiar about the eyes.'

'You'll need to be pretty certain of your facts before you start making accusations like that, Ellie. If you are wrong, he could sue you for slander, defamation of character and all that.'

'Well, how am I supposed to do that? I wouldn't know where to start.'

'Well, gut instinct is not sufficient,' he replied, draining his glass and standing up. 'Look, I'd better be getting back, but, listen, I have to go to Nairobi for a few days to see someone about the animal centre and to pick up a consignment of veterinary drugs and some radio collars. I know some police friends there. I may be able to get some information about Max Hooper and Ryder Leason. Don't get your hopes up though. It's just an enquiry. We'll see what comes up, if anything.'

'Would you do that for me?' Ellie asked. 'And would the police help?'

'I can but try, anything for my girl,' he said, kissing her good-night and slipping silently out of the tent.

She heard the noise of the zip and he was gone. Was she his girl then, she thought. She still wasn't sure if it had been a good idea getting involved again. Their future looked difficult. Would she be able to trust him fully?

And there was still the question of Kim Wakahki. Were they an item? A cold finger of doubt crept over her and she shivered. Why did life get so complicated just when you had things all mapped out?

The next morning, tables and chairs had been set out in the clearing beside the remains of the previous night's campfire and they all enjoyed a cooked breakfast overlooking the river. Then the buses would leave the site for the remainder of the safari. Tom had drunk a fair bit the previous night and although he wasn't suffering a hang-over, he had drunk enough to ensure he didn't notice Ellie's pensive mood.

This made the rest of the day amicable between them and Tom still snapped away at all the wildlife as though the Nesbitt and Britten Image Library was a going concern. Ellie didn't want to think about it. She couldn't get Harrison out of her mind.

Tom wasn't one for sunbathing, so Ellie was dozing on a sunbed by herself the day after they had returned from the exhausting safari trip. Tom had gone off in search of some fishing activity, and more photo opportunities, no doubt.

'Hi, Ellie,' a syrupy voice sang out.

Ellie opened her eyes and squinted out from under her arm to see Cameo standing in front of her in a bikini that looked as though it were made entirely from string and wearing nothing else except the infamous mermaid locket and sunglasses.

'Has Tom abandoned you? I know the feeling.'

'He's gone fishing,' Ellie replied.

'Men just can't sit still for very long, can they?'

'Actually, Tom and I . . . well . . . we aren't . . . '

She didn't finish the sentence and Cameo wasn't really listening. She was pulling a sunbed closer to Ellie's and talking to a waiter in Swahili, ordering drinks.

'I'll leave my bag here,' she told Ellie. 'I'm just going to swim a few lengths before I lie out in the sun.'

She had Ellie's full attention as she unclasped the mermaid locket from her neck and pushed it inside her beach-bag.

'Yes, sure,' Ellie said, her eyes firmly on the bag.

'I'll be back shortly,' Cameo said and

91

walked down the steps of the pool at the shallow end. She proceeded to swim gracefully away from Ellie towards the deep end without getting her hair wet or losing the sun-glasses that were now perched on top of her head.

Ellie didn't need to think about it twice. She reached into Cameo's bag and pulled out the locket. She stared at it and just knew that it was the exact same one that had been her mother's. The weight of it, the feel of it, every contour of the jewel-encrusted mermaid, and inside? She snapped it open and there were the words she had known would be there — **All My Love R**.

Her father, Roger, had had this engraved especially for her mother, Adrienne. Ellie closed the locket and laid it in the palm of her hand. She must have been staring at it for more than just a few minutes as she pictured her mother's smiling face with the locket at her throat. Tears threatened to spill over but she blinked them away quickly as she was brought back sharply to the present.

Cameo had picked up her towel from the next sun-bed and was towelling herself dry.

'It's beautiful, isn't it?' she said to Ellie. 'Ryder had it specially made for me, for our engagement. He is such a romantic. He's even had it engraved.'

She took it from Ellie and snapped it open.

'All my love R,' she read out.

'Why didn't he put his full name?' Ellie asked her.

Cameo laughed as she fixed it back round her neck. She patted it against her throat.

'This way is far more intriguing and romantic. Besides, I know it's from him.'

Just then, they were interrupted by sounds of laughing and back-slapping.

'Well done. How big was it? Didn't I see you at the fish market this morning?'

Ellie and Cameo looked up and

Cameo's face widened into a big grin. She waved to Ryder.

'Hi, babe, we're over here.'

Ellie watched as Ryder came sauntering towards them with Tom at his side, looking like the cat that got the cream. He'd obviously had some success on the fishing trip. A few paces behind them both was Vince and a red-faced Ernest, puffing and panting and mopping his brow with a large white handkerchief.

'I caught a sail-fish, bigger than me it was.'

Tom couldn't wait to tell them all about it. Ellie tried not to stare at Ryder Leason, although he didn't seem to realise who she was. If indeed he was Max, he obviously didn't recognise her.

'What's this?'

She laughed.

'Are you telling tall fishermen's tales now? Hi, Ernest, you're looking a bit hot. Come and sit in the shade.'

'I'll get us some cold drinks,' Vince said, waving at a nearby waiter collecting empty glasses.

Ryder bent down and kissed Cameo.

'This man is a natural,' he said and pointed to Tom. 'His first time fishing and he's beaten the record for this month already. We've written it up on the board at the clubhouse.'

'Excellent, Tom,' Ellie said. 'Well done.'

He'd put behind him the embarrassing revelation from the day before and nodded amicably.

The drinks arrived and they all sat at a table underneath a shady palm, but Ellie's thoughts drifted from the conversation taking place around her. Was she wrong in thinking Ryder was really the crooked Max Hooper? Everyone seemed to be very friendly with him here, including Ernest. She wracked her brain trying to remember if Ernest would ever have been at her father's offices when Max had been there.

She was desperate to talk to someone about her suspicions. But it was all only a hunch. There was no concrete evidence and if she started throwing accusations around that were untrue, well, as Harrison had said, she could be letting herself in for some big trouble. She had to wait for Harrison first to see if he'd managed to find out anything. Cameo had been right, she did feel abandoned, but not by Tom. She was experiencing the pang of loss that Harrison's absence had caused.

She listened to the others droning on and hoped that neither Tom nor Vince would mention who she really was, or talk about her parents in front of Ryder because she had a sudden menacing premonition. There was some unfinished business afoot, of that she was certain.

6

The boat moved effortlessly through the turquoise waters of the Indian Ocean, the reflection of the sun gently wavering over the surface like floating golden leaves. Three dolphins were riding the bow waves, just a few feet from the hull, their timing precise and unerring. It could have been described as a perfect day, but Ellie was disturbed.

The previous afternoon, after Tom's magnificent sail-fish catch, Ryder had invited them to come out for a relaxing sail on his yacht, Simba. At first Ellie had thought it would be a good chance to find out some more about him and confirm her suspicions, but she had woken up in the night feeling apprehensive and now that they were out here at sea with the land receding in the distance, she had a distinctly uneasy feeling. Something wasn't right but she couldn't quite put her finger on what it was that was making her feel so peculiar.

Ellie sat in the corner of the centre cockpit and watched them all drinking beers and laughing and joking together. Ryder was at the helm with Cameo hanging round his waist, nibbling unashamedly at his earlobe. Tom was looking quite pleased with himself, too. Kim had turned up at the hotel that morning and had been invited to come along for the trip and was hanging on to his every word.

Tom's got over me very quickly, Ellie thought as he flirted with Kim quite openly in front of her. Kim was obviously quite attracted to him, too, so maybe she didn't have any designs on Harrison after all. Ellie felt a bit left out, with Harrison still not back from Nairobi yet, and she wished that Ernest had accepted the sailing invitation, too, instead of pleading that he was a landlubber. She could have done with his company for support. She and Tom, after being such good friends, seemed miles apart today.

'You're looking a bit green,' Ryder commented. 'Have you not been sailing before?'

'No,' Ellie started to lie.

'Come off it,' Tom said unwittingly. 'I thought you used to sail with your parents.'

Ellie threw him a warning look.

'That was many years ago, Tom, when I was quite young, and I didn't actually do any of the sailing. I wouldn't know a mainsail from a genoa to save my life.'

'I've never even heard of a genoa,' Kim put in.

'I think it's the big one at the front,' Tom replied.

'Your parents have a yacht, then?' Ryder said. 'What type is it?'

This was exactly the conversation that Ellie wanted to avoid. She realised how stupid she had been to come sailing today. How she wished she had waited back at the hotel until Harrison had got back to see if he had found out anything about Ryder.

'Oh, I've no idea,' Ellie was flippant. 'Similar to this, I suppose. One's much the same as the next when you're a child.'

She felt herself turning red. She was never good at lying, but she had no wish to elaborate. Ryder was giving her a rather strange look, or was she imagining it?

Then Cameo, in her usual dizzy way, perked up and joined in the conversation.

'Ellie's parents are dead, honey. You remember those people killed on their yacht out here?' she said, totally oblivious at how inappropriate and insensitive this statement was.

Ryder turned to her, his eyebrows raised.

'Really?' he said.

Cameo continued blindly.

'Well, I think she's really brave doing this. I arranged some flowers for her, darling, and Vince took her and Tom out on the launch, to conduct a kind of memorial service.'

Ellie started to feel sick again as the conversation was totally out of her control now.

'I do remember something about an English couple being murdered on their yacht,' he said thoughtfully, 'a few years back, awful business. That was your parents, was it? You poor thing. Is that why you're out here, to hold a memorial service?'

'Not really.'

Ellie tried to rescue the situation.

'Ernest Grey is my godfather,' she went on, trying to keep her voice steady. 'Tom and I are just here on a working holiday and visiting him. I thought the flowers would be a nice tribute to make at the same time.'

She was staring at Ryder, trying to decide how sincere he really was.

'Sure,' Ryder said, his eyes half on her, half on the set of the sails. 'Did they ever catch who did it?'

Ellie could feel herself getting more and more distressed.

'No,' she said abruptly. 'I doubt we'll ever know. Excuse me, I must go below.'

She started to make a move towards the hatch leading down to the main saloon area and bathroom area. Tom realised he'd made Ellie feel uncomfortable by correcting her. It should have been obvious to him that it was a subject she would not have wanted raised.

'Sorry, Ellie,' he said as she passed him, 'not very tactful of me, and I'm sure Cameo didn't realise what she was saying. Are you OK?'

'Please, don't worry. I'll be fine in a minute,' she assured him.

Tom had no idea what was going on inside her head and she tried to play it down.

'I'm just feeling a bit seasick, that's all. No harm done.'

She caught Ryder's eye briefly as she swung herself down inside the hatch and started down the companionway. Was he now suspicious of her intentions? She wasn't sure how to describe the look he gave her, but he didn't look friendly. His eyes penetrated hers and just for a second they were dark and sinister.

Ellie stared round the inside of the cabin, her eyes getting used to the gloom after the glare of the sun. There were heavy maroon curtains pulled across the portholes, casting a strange, soft glow. They kept the sun out, but nevertheless it was hot and stuffy down there. The boat was leaning to port, and Ellie adjusted her feet on the slope of the boards and held on as she edged past the galley.

The cooker squeaked slightly as it rocked backwards and forwards. There was a gurgle from the wastepipe in the kitchen sink and the sound of waves slapping against the side of the hull, familiar noises that transported Ellie right back to her parents' yacht and far from not really remembering it as she had tried to convince Ryder, she remembered every single inch of it, every nook and cranny, every creak and groan.

It all felt so familiar, this could have been the same yacht. As she walked past the crescent-shaped seating area she glanced up at the lamp swinging backwards and forwards above the table. Without questioning her actions, she lifted up the corner of one of the seating cushions. The distant memories hurtled down the corridors of time and mixed with the present as Ellie struggled with her emotions.

There it was, quite worn and faint, but definitely there, at the back, just where she knew she would find it. She ran her fingers over the tiny mermaid, crudely carved into the woodwork that supported the seating. It was a simple carving made with a small penknife — Ellie's penknife, with the mother-of-pearl handle, a present from her father.

Feeling bored one afternoon, she had carved it herself. She'd been fourteen years old. Back then the vessel had been called Calypso Mermaid and it had been her father at the helm, not Ryder Leason. The walls started to close in around Ellie and her head was pounding fit to burst. She reached the toilet and locked herself in. She pumped some cold water into the small sink and splashed her face. Then she sat down and put her face down between her knees. After a few minutes the feeling of nausea had passed, but now Ellie was shivering.

This could all mean only one thing. This was her parents' yacht! The question was, had Ryder bought it perfectly innocently? If not, then did he have something to do with their murder? Footsteps passed outside the porthole at Ellie's eye level. She watched as Ryder's deck shoes moved past and she stifled a gasp.

She knew she couldn't stay locked in here until they got back to the marina. How on earth was she going to act normally with so many unanswered questions burning in her head? With all these facts it looked like too much of a coincidence. Ellie took a deep breath and tried to decide what to do. She knew already that she couldn't just burst out into the cockpit and start throwing accusations around with no proof. She had to play it cool, act normally and keep calm until they were back on dry land. Then she'd wait for Harrison. He would know what to do.

If Ryder was Max Hooper he was a dangerous conman. He wouldn't be the type of man to get on the wrong side of, especially out at sea. If he was also a murderer, who knows what lengths he would go to, to make sure he was not brought to justice.

Ellie mustered all the composure she possibly could for the rest of the sailing trip and climbed back out into the cockpit.

They got back to the marina at three o'clock in the afternoon and Ryder drove them back to the hotel. Much to Ellie's disappointment Harrison had not yet returned, there was no message from him either and at Vince's invitation Ryder was joining them for drinks on the terrace.

'Thank you for taking us out today,' Kim said. 'I really enjoyed it.'

She was standing very close to Tom as he agreed.

'Yeah, it was great of you to spare the time.'

'No problem,' Ryder said. 'I enjoyed it, too. What about you, Ellie? Did you have a good time after you got your sea legs back?'

It was hard, but Ellie forced a smile and nodded.

'Yes, I did. Thank you, but I'm glad to be back on dry land. I think I am more of a landlubber, like Ernest.'

'Maybe I could take you out again before you return to England,' Ryder said, an innocent offer, but to Ellie it sounded more like a threat.

The waiter arrived with their drinks and Ellie sat quietly sipping hers while the others carried on their conversation.

She was waiting for the right time to make her excuses and go back to her chalet, plead a headache or something. But just as she was about to politely excuse herself, Kim suddenly jumped up.

'Oh, I nearly forgot, my photograph albums! I brought them along this morning to show you.'

This was directed more at Tom than Ellie.

'Where did you put them, Vince?'

'Behind the bar,' Vince told her and called Jacob, the bar manager, to fetch them over.

Kim had arrived armed with them that morning as the others were preparing to leave for the sailing trip. She had left them in Vince's safekeeping when Ryder had invited her to join them. Ellie knew it wouldn't be polite to leave the group yet so she accepted another drink and settled down to look at Kim's snaps. Kim was looking coyly at Tom from beneath her long dark lashes.

'Maybe you could use these in your image library, Tom. I prefer to photograph people, as you can see,' she told him, flicking over the pages. 'These are of the Masai tribes, and these are fishermen, mending their nets.'

Tom was impressed.

'These are very good,' he said. 'No, seriously, you've a real talent. Look at these, Ellie. The colour, the angles, the way you use the light . . . '

Tom was off on his favourite subject. He passed the book to Ellie.

'Look at the way Kim's caught the vibrant colours of the market. It just comes to life.'

Ellie started looking at them, trying to feign interest until one in particular jumped out at her and she suddenly gave a little gasp.

'What is it?' Vince said. 'Are you all right?'

'I think I've been bitten,' Ellie lied and bent her head down towards her ankle and started to inspect her skin for signs of the non-existent bite.

How could Ellie explain to everyone that one of the pictures in Kim's album was of her parents shopping in a Kenyan market? She couldn't, not in front of Ryder. It was always supposed that they had not landed in Kenya, murdered at sea by pirates before they ever set foot in the country. This put a new light on everything and Ellie needed time to think.

A waiter came over.

'A call for Miss Britten,' he said. 'You can use the phone at the bar.'

It was just the diversion Ellie needed.

'Excuse me,' she said as she left the table quickly without looking at Ryder.

She bent down to rub her ankle and continue the pretence of a painful insect bite. It must be Harrison on the phone. It had to be, she thought, as she picked up the receiver. The line was terrible. It crackled and popped.

'Hello . . . Harrison?'

'Hi, Ellie. Yes, it's me. Can you hear me? This line's awful.'

'Isn't it! I can only just hear you.

Where are you? You're not still in Nairobi?'

'No, I'm in Mombasa.'

The line clicked again.

'Hello, are you still there?'

'Yes. When will you be back? How did things go? Any luck?'

The line coughed and spluttered yet again and Ellie was worried that it was about to disconnect.

'My blasted truck won't start,' Harrison cursed. 'I'm going to be a while yet, but they say they can fix it. I'll be back after one o'clock though. I'll come straight to your chalet. I've . . . got . . . some . . . '

Ellie strained her ears.

'You've got what? Hello? Are you there, hello?'

Harrison sounded as though he was talking to someone in the background.

'I'll have to go, Ellie. I'll see you later. Are you OK?'

'Yes, I'm fine. Something has happened here, though. I'll tell you when you get back. I miss you.'

'I . . . too,' Harrison was saying something else but Ellie was unable to decipher it through the crackling on the line.

Then the line went dead, and Ellie stood there staring at the receiver. She put it back down on its cradle and stood there for a few moments. The sound of his voice had filled her momentarily with confidence, but suddenly she felt totally alone.

Just out of eyesight, behind a pillar, Ryder finished eavesdropping on her call and walked off towards the men's toilets as Ellie made her way back to the table outside on the terrace and told the others she was going to lie down for a while before dinner. She looked round for Ryder, frowning.

'He'll be back in a minute,' Cameo told her.

'Tell him, thank you again for today.'

Ellie smiled, but as she walked away from the table the smile died on her lips and she looked about uneasily.

The evening was not a relaxed one.

Kim joined her and Tom for dinner and the atmosphere was awkward. Ellie felt like a gooseberry but she needed company. She felt very vulnerable after today and didn't want to be left alone. She wanted to ask Kim about the photo in her album, if she remembered taking it and when? But Ellie was reluctant to talk to anyone about her suspicions of Ryder.

The fewer people who knew, the better, she thought and soon Harrison would be back. So she endured a strained evening until she couldn't stand it anymore and said good-night, leaving Tom and Kim by themselves. Ellie could feel the vibes between them and it made her miss Harrison even more. Well, if Tom got together with Kim she'd at least feel less guilty, even though she was a bit miffed that he appeared to have forgotten how he had felt about her earlier in the week and had found a replacement companion so quickly.

Ellie hurried along the dark path

towards the chalets. The moon cast strange shadows of the trees across the grass ahead of her and she jumped every time she heard the sound of an insect. She was still going over all the events of the past few days and trying to make sense of everything.

Now that Tom had told Ryder who she was, would Ryder assume that she now knew who he was, if he was Max Hooper at all? Was she in danger? Maybe she was mistaken and this was all just her vivid imagination running away with her.

However, the more she analysed events the more things sounded likely. If Ellie's parents had made it to Kenya, and while visiting had bumped into Max Hooper, alias Ryder, he may have murdered them and made it look like pirates. He could have stolen Calypso Mermaid, refurbished it and called it Simba and given the locket to Cameo because it very conveniently had his initial inside it and would make a wonderful engagement present.

Ellie was bitter that all Ryder's wealth could have grown from money he had embezzled from her father. It all sounded so plausible. Everything fitted, but there was still no proof. Had Harrison found out anything? She prayed he had something. She had to avenge her parents' death, get back what was rightfully hers and bring the murderer to justice.

As she neared the chalet, her heart started to beat faster. Suppose someone was lurking in the shadows, lying in wait for her — one of Ryder's henchmen. Surely he wouldn't try anything in the hotel. He'd never get away with it. She looked about her furtively and when she reached the door, fumbled, shaking, trying to get the key into the lock. The hairs prickled on the back of her neck. She opened the door. It was pitch dark inside.

Didn't I leave a light on, she asked herself as she stepped inside and flicked the light switch. She quickly shut the door behind her and locked it. Leaning on it, she waited for her heartbeat to return to normal, listening. A tap dripped in the bathroom making her jump again. She took a deep breath and then checked behind the shower curtain, the wardrobe, under the bed. What was happening to her? She was a nervous wreck.

She lay down on the bed fully clothed and watched the clock as it ticked towards midnight.

7

Vince was a very generous guy. He handed a key to Kim, saying, 'It's too late to be driving back by yourself. Stay here tonight. There's a spare chalet.'

'Oh, are you sure?' Kim said, surprised. 'That's very kind of you. I hadn't planned to stay so long.'

As Vince bade them good-night, Kim turned towards Tom and dangled the key under his nose.

'Fancy a nightcap, Tom?' she purred.

By one o'clock, the hotel was winding down and by half past it was all but deserted. Ellie was sleeping, but fitfully, still fully dressed. She didn't hear the spare hotel key turning in the lock or see the dark hand reach in and switch off the main light that she had left on. The silent figure in the doorway waited while Ellie stirred restlessly and turned over. She didn't wake but was now facing the wall, away from the door.

The figure pushed the door open farther and it swung inwards quietly. A light breeze blew into the chalet and the air-conditioning machine changed speed automatically. The figure beckoned to his accomplice. Stealthily they crept across the room towards Ellie, their shoes squeaking slightly on the tiled floor.

The first one reached Ellie's bed, and pulled back the mosquito net. He paused just long enough to admire her long blonde hair fanned out on the pillow before he stretched out his arms and pushed the rag of ether against Ellie's mouth and nose. She was instantly awake and immediately struggled and as she realised what was happening to her, her eyes widened with fear.

Her lungs began to ache as she fought for air and she put her arms up and grabbed hold of the man's wrists with both hands, pulling and scratching at him, but her futile attempts began to fail as the ether started to envelop her. The man was immensely powerful and Ellie stayed awake just long enough to feel the muscles tense like rock in his forearm before she lost consciousness and fell back on to the pillow.

Satisfied, the two men whispered to each other in Swahili before bundling Ellie into a sheet they had pulled from the bed. Then she was picked up and thrown over one of the men's shoulders like a limp rag doll. As they made their way back across the room Ellie's feet were sticking out, accidentally knocking over the chair by the dressing table. It clattered noisily on the tiled floor, the sound echoing through the wall into the chalet next door. Unfortunately, Tom was not there to hear it.

After a quick look outside, the two men, together with their human parcel, slipped silently around the side of the building and made their way across a piece of wasteland behind the hotel kitchens. They crossed an expanse of grass and through a gate, and they were outside the grounds where a Land-Rover was waiting with its engine running and its lights switched off.

Ellie was bundled unceremoniously into the back and as the men climbed in, a third man let out the clutch and gently coaxed the vehicle down the seldom-used rough track.

★ ★ ★

Harrison had finally managed to get his truck going and had driven from Mombasa to Kilifi in record time, although the potholes hadn't done his suspension much good. He was eager to see Ellie again. What had she been talking about when she had told him something had happened today? He wished he hadn't had to cut their conversation short and hoped that she hadn't been doing any sleuthing by herself and getting into trouble.

He had been doing a lot of thinking about her these past few days. He had a good feeling about their future but first he had to talk to her about what had really happened ten years ago and he knew it wouldn't be easy.

It was three in the morning as he pulled up in the parking area outside the hotel. The main doors were closed but the light was on and the side door was ajar leading into the manager's office. Harrison poked his head round the door. Two night security guards were playing cards in the smoke-filled room. They knew Harrison well so waved him through with a wink when he told them he'd come to see a friend.

He walked through the silent hotel and made his way to Ellie's chalet. He knew something was wrong as soon as he caught sight of the open door and the chair on its side. His stomach sank when he saw that there had been a struggle. A sheet was missing, the mosquito net torn from its pole and he was aware of a funny smell. He bent down, picked up the piece of rag by the bed and sniffed it. Ether!

Harrison pushed his hand through

his hair. Ellie's bag and purse were on the dressing-table so it wasn't theft. This was not good, not good at all.

Was it possible that she had been kidnapped? How on earth had Ellie managed to get herself into this mess? Were her suspicions right after all? Was Ryder really Max Hooper? The police had been helpful enough in Nairobi but these things took time, more time than he had been able to spare and he had left before anything had come through from the UK. He thought for a moment that if tonight's drama was down to Ryder, Ellie most probably would be taken to the marina. What would Ryder do to her? Harrison went cold at the thought that he might be too late.

He needed Tom's help. He stepped over the foot-high fence to Tom's chalet. Knocking on his door he called out, but there was no answer. Harrison peered through a gap in the curtains. He could see that Tom's bed hadn't been slept in. He wasn't there. What was going on?

He was running out of time. He had to work fast and get to the marina before anything happened to Ellie. For one horrible moment he thought that perhaps Tom had been with Ellie. No! Surely not. He couldn't bear to think of the two of them together and the fact that he could be mistaken about Ellie and how she felt about him. But there was no time to speculate on the relationship. If they had been together maybe they had both been kidnapped. There was no time to lose.

Harrison made his way back outside to his truck. The security guards were no longer in the office. They had chosen a very inopportune moment to go off and do their rounds of the hotel and its grounds. Harrison couldn't waste the time trying to locate them. He jumped into his truck and sped off down the hotel drive kicking up dust and gravel as he spun out on to the main road. He clutched the steering wheel tightly and stared ahead with grim determination in the direction of the marina.

The main gates to the marina were closed when he arrived. Harrison cut the engine and coasted down the slope past them stopping a little farther down the track. Making his way on foot down the side of the fence he found a place that wasn't too difficult to scale. He was thankful that Ryder had no vicious dogs guarding the premises but wondered what alternative security there was. As he jumped down the other side, he held his breath, waiting for alarms to go off and floodlights to illuminate him.

There were none. Harrison looked around to get his bearings. Making his way past the clubhouse towards the single-storey residence that Ryder shared with Cameo, he tried to decide what to do when he got there. He had no proof that Ryder was involved with Ellie's kidnap. On the other hand, if Ryder had somehow found out that Ellie recognised him from the past then it was the most likely explanation. He looked around and listened. Where was

Ellie? Was she close by hurt, tied up, frightened?

He felt a sudden pain of longing for her deep inside him. She did mean something to him, he was sure of that and it was almost too much to contemplate that something bad might have happened to her.

The low white-painted bungalow loomed ahead. It was in total darkness but as Harrison got nearer he could see that none of the blinds or curtains had been drawn across. It looked deserted. He crept stealthily from one window to another, peering in at the expensively-furnished rooms. He could see there was no-one inside. However, when he got to the master bedroom he could see Cameo asleep in a big four-poster. He watched the rise and fall of her breathing through the mosquito net that hung round the bed and noted that she was alone. Harrison frowned. Where was Ryder? And what was he up to in the middle of the night?

Harrison trod carefully around the

dry path surrounding the building and walked down the slope to the edge of the creek, turning his attention to the small man-made harbour where Ryder Leason moored his fleet of tourist cruisers and yachts. Moving silently in the shadows, he scoured the vessels for any signs of life. The gentle breeze rattled the rigging in the yachts and the halyards twanged faintly.

Harrison was about to move away when a muted light on board a large ketch farther along the moorings caught his eye and sounds of movement in the cabin had his full attention. He moved towards the beautiful, twin-masted vessel. It was called Simba, Swahili for lion and he knew it was Ryder's favourite yacht.

The light was coming from the forward section of the yacht. At the rear, behind the cockpit, the aft cabin was in darkness and Harrison decided that if Ellie and Tom were tied up on board, they would probably be locked in that one. It seemed logical. Harrison crept nearer towards the vessel. He knew that if he tried to get on board by walking up the gangplank he would probably be heard, but as far as he could see there was no other way.

He stood on the gangplank and edged his way along it, trying not to go too fast and announce his arrival. He stepped down quietly into the cockpit and listened, aware that he had been holding his breath. He crept around the side of the aft cabin and bent down, peering into the nearest porthole. The curtains were pulled across and he couldn't see. He swore under his breath.

Looking at the hatch he could see that there was a padlock hanging off the opening hinge. Were they both locked in there? As he pondered what to do next, the hatch on the forward cabin was pulled back and Ryder Leason's head appeared at the top of the companion-way. He had obviously been drinking and didn't look his usual debonair self. In fact he looked extremely agitated, unshaven and his dark eyebrows seemed closer together making him appear altogether very menacing.

'Well, good evening, Harrison, or rather, should I say good morning? What on earth brings you out here at this time? You do realise that it's three-thirty in the morning, don't you? A bit late for socialising.'

Ryder was eyeing Harrison very warily but not as yet giving anything away. Harrison tried to play it cool.

'I've been looking for you. There's an emergency up at the hotel,' he said. 'Ellie and Tom are missing and we need all the help we can get. We think they may have been kidnapped.'

Ryder showed no reaction at all.

'Kidnapped, you say, from the hotel? I hardly think that is likely. They probably went canoodling on the beach and fell asleep down there. I'd wait until morning before you raise the alarm, mate.'

Harrison watched him carefully.

'If that is the case, I don't think Ellie

would have messed up her chalet, kicked over a chair and smothered herself with ether before going out and leaving the door open, do you?'

'How did you get in here? The main gate was locked,' Ryder said, ignoring Harrison's last remark.

Harrison felt that his suspicions were grounded.

'Have you seen the pair of them tonight?' he persisted.

Ryder was immediately on the defensive.

'What are you implying? You think I had something to do with it? Why on earth would you think that?'

Beads of sweat were glistening on Ryder's forehead and he pushed his hand through his floppy fringe and wiped his forehead on his arm.

'I've no idea,' Harrison said slowly. 'Perhaps we should ask Max Hooper.'

Ryder seemed momentarily disadvantaged, but at that point a creaking on the gangplank heralded the arrival of the two burly Kenyans and Ryder regained his authority. He and Harrison eyed each other angrily as the two hench-men stood by, waiting for instructions.

'Just say the word, boss. He'll be shark meat.'

Behind Harrison in the aft cabin there was a sudden noise. It sounded as though someone was kicking on the side of the bulkheads.

'Ellie,' Harrison shouted. 'Tom, is that you?'

He picked up a wooden boat hook from the deck as Ryder laughed.

'Oh, dear, my friend, I'm afraid you are going to have to join your lady-friend now. Too bad, eh?'

Harrison swung round and made a lunge for Ryder with the hook end of the pole but the two Kenyans were coming towards him before he could get there. Harrison took a step back-wards, brandishing the boat hook like a Samurai sword. He caught one of the men in his eye and as the wounded man held his face in his hands, groaning, the other one lost his balance and fell overboard into the creek as Harrison gave him two hefty whacks over the head.

Ryder had gone down below, and he came back out brandishing a gun. As Harrison reached out and tried to grab at it, it went off and caught Harrison in the shoulder. He fell back into the cockpit clutching his arm and grimacing with the pain. Ryder stood over him.

'Now that was very stupid of you,' Ryder sneered.

The first henchman stood beside him now still holding his face where the boat hook had left a nasty crimson gash from his eyelid to his ear. The second man had dragged himself out of the water and rejoined his mate and Ryder, dripping, in the cockpit.

'Tie him up and throw him into the cabin with the girl,' Ryder ordered his men.

They obeyed without speaking then unlocked the hatch. Harrison found himself tumbling down into the cabin like a sack of coal.

8

Ellie was lying on one of the bunks with her hands and feet tied. She looked up nervously as the hatch was opened and Harrison tumbled into the cabin. He lay in a crumpled heap on the wooden deck below her and she could see he was badly hurt. A crimson patch was spread across his shirt and he was barely conscious.

The hatch closed again and Ellie heard the rattle of the padlock.

'Harrison!' she cried. 'What have they done to you?'

There was no reply. Ellie wriggled her hands and feet. It was useless. The cords bit into her wrists and ankles and her shoulders ached from being pulled behind her. The tears began to flow again and dripped on to the pillow beneath her head.

Harrison had been the one thought

in her mind since the ether had worn off and she had realised the predicament she was in. She had hoped against hope that he had managed to get some incriminating evidence from his police friend in Nairobi and that he would arrive with help, her knight in shining armour, and she would be rescued. Now, as she looked down at him, wounded and unconscious, she admitted to herself that that scenario was the things of movies. In reality they were both in serious trouble and she felt it was all her fault. She looked around the cabin and wracked her brains trying to think of a plan of action, some way of escape.

It must have been over an hour later that she heard Harrison groan. He tried to shift and move his weight off his shoulder, but another flash of pain shot through his body and Ellie was frantic.

'Harrison, wake up! It's me, Ellie. Can you hear me?'

Harrison opened his eyes a fraction and looked up at her. His face was ashen, and dark rings had appeared beneath his eyes.

'Ellie,' he croaked.

Tears of relief that he was at least alive filled Ellie's eyes.

'Thank goodness,' she said. 'I thought they'd killed you.'

'They'll have to do better than that,' Harrison joked, then winced with pain again. 'Where's Tom?'

Ellie frowned.

'Tom?'

Harrison's breathing was heavy. He was reluctant to admit to Ellie that he had thought they'd been together.

'I went to your room but you were gone. I went to get Tom and he wasn't in his room either. I thought they had taken both of you.'

'I don't know where he is, but he's not here,' Ellie said and a flicker of hope entered her mind.

Maybe Tom would get help, when he found her missing in the morning.

'What have they done to you? I heard the shot. I was so scared,' Ellie went on, powerless to help him.

'I'm caught in the shoulder, and it hurts. What about you? Are you OK? They didn't hurt you?'

She dismissed her own welfare.

'Did you get anything on Ryder from your police contacts? Any proof that he's Max Hooper?'

Harrison took another deep breath.

'They're sending something through to the hotel by fax as soon as they get anything back from the UK. You know how long these things take.'

'That's not going to help us now anyway, is it? It's obvious he's a crook,' Ellie stated resignedly. 'The question is, what is he going to do with us now?'

As though in answer to her question, the in-board engine suddenly throbbed into life and there was the sound of mooring ropes being thrown down on the deck. The boat was leaving her berth.

'Oh, no! He's going to take us out to sea, isn't he? He's going to murder us just like he murdered my parents.'

Ellie was hysterical. Harrison summoned all the energy he could muster.

'Ellie! Pull yourself together. We can get out of this. There must be a way. We can't just lie here and wait for the inevitable.'

'How on earth are we going to escape this?'

'We'll have to try and break out of the hatch or the skylight. First we must get untied. Can you swing your legs down behind me? I can try and undo the cord.'

'I'll try,' Ellie replied.

She looked briefly up at the padlock dangling down from the skylight, hiding her doubt that they could open it. She started to wriggle down the bunk towards him.

She slid her legs over the side. Ignoring the pain in her shoulder blades, she shuffled her backside to the edge of the bunk and pushed her feet up behind Harrison. His fingers groped around for the ends of the cord. As he felt for the knot and started working it loose, the pain in his shoulder increased and seared through him like someone twisting a hot knife into his flesh. Sweat was pouring off him as he concentrated what little strength he had into the job at hand. He tried to take his mind off the pain.

'Ellie, what was it that happened yesterday? On the phone last night, you said something had happened.'

Ellie exhaled.

'Ryder took us out on his yacht for a sail, myself, Tom, Kim and Cameo. I didn't feel well though. I thought I was just sea-sick. Tom and Cameo started talking about my parents, you know, about what happened. Ryder was acting really strange. He kept giving me odd looks, like he knew exactly who I was and that I knew his real identity.'

Harrison shook his head.

'You shouldn't have gone. He's a very dangerous man.'

'I know that,' Ellie replied, indignantly. 'I don't know why I did, but that's not all.'

'There's more?'

Ellie dropped her bombshell.

'This yacht, Simba. It's not Simba at all. It's my parent's boat, the Calypso Mermaid, the one they left England in to sail round the world.'

Harrison stared at Ellie incredulously.

'You're sure?'

'Positive. I found a carving of a mermaid under the seat in the saloon. I did it when I was fourteen.'

'Oh, my God,' Harrison whispered.

'We're in real trouble, aren't we?' Ellie stated the obvious.

By the time the Calypso Mermaid had reached the mouth of the creek and open sea, daylight was just appearing on the horizon and Ellie's feet had been released.

'Can you squat down behind me now?' Harrison asked. 'I'll try and untie your wrists.'

Ellie slid off the bunk and sat on the floor next to him. Harrison's legs were facing the hatch and Ellie's, now

138

thankfully free, were facing the rear bulkhead. She could see Harrison's wound was still bleeding profusely. They both sat staring at each other for a moment in the confined spaces of the floor-well. Harrison found it difficult to move.

Ellie leaned forward and kissed his lips. His skin was cold and clammy. He was feverish, and she hoped he would last out until they were rescued. She had to face the fact that escape was not looking very probable at the moment. Harrison could barely move, let alone get the hatch open.

'I love you, Ellie,' he said unexpectedly.

Her heart missed a beat. All thought of her job in England and her and Tom's business venture left her mind. All she could think about was the present and a prayer that she and Harrison would get through this alive to contemplate a future together.

'We are going to make it, aren't we?' she said.

'Of course we are.'

Ellie shuffled herself forward until they were sitting back to back. She knew how much pain he was causing himself by moving his arms, but he worked as hard as he could to release her wrists. As the cords fell away and her shoulders jerked forward, Ellie cried out in pain. The cramp was almost unbearable. They sat in silence for a few moments as Ellie rubbed her shoulders and wrists and tried to get her circulation back to normal.

'Now you,' she said.

It was easier for Ellie with both hands free and she soon had the cords off. Harrison was starting to shiver now and Ellie felt a surge of emotion rush over her as she stared down at him. She had to be strong. He looked so helpless that she just wanted to take him in her arms and rock him.

'We must get you up on the bunk and get a blanket round you, and find something to staunch the bullet wound and support your arm.'

Ellie surprised herself by suddenly taking over the situation. She looked around the cabin for some inspiration.

'Oh, my goodness,' she said. 'I wonder . . . '

She started scrabbling inside the locker that ran around the cabin just above the bunks. Harrison was watching her. His exertion had left him exhausted and he was resting his head against the side of the bunk as Ellie pulled a piece of plywood sideways out of the locker and then put her hand back in. She felt around the small cavity underneath.

'What are you doing?' Harrison asked curiously.

'Eureka,' Ellie said triumphantly, and held up a little penknife with a mother-of-pearl handle. 'This was my cabin when I was young, and that was my secret hiding place for treasures.'

She nodded towards the locker, then held up the little pen-knife.

'We can use this to break open the skylight.'

'Clever girl.'

Harrison managed a small smile, then winced again as he moved his shoulder. Working quickly and more confident now that she had something positive to do, Ellie pulled the sheet off the bunk and using the penknife she sliced up some strips. She rolled some up into a pad then bent down to open Harrison's shirt and administer some first aid to his wound.

'Ripping my shirt off again,' Harrison said with a twinkle in his eye, remembering the passion they had shared at the Moja camp.

'How can you joke at a time like this?' Ellie scolded. 'Keep still. This might hurt.'

The boat started swaying more as the hull cut its way through the waves and headed farther out to sea.

After ten minutes of Ellie's gentle nursing, Harrison was feeling a little more comfortable. Ellie had pressed pads of sheeting against his wound and used some more as a bandage around his chest and shoulder to keep it in place. Then she had made a sling to support his arm and with his help had managed to get him on to the bunk, leaning back against several pillows.

She pulled the blanket up over him.

'I really need a drink,' he said, licking his dry lips.

'There's nothing in here,' Ellie told him. 'I've looked.'

It was hot in the cabin, and he'd lost a lot of blood. Ellie knew he would get dehydrated very quickly if he didn't get a drink. She tried not to think too far ahead. They both had to get out of here. The alternative was not an option. Ellie took the little pen-knife and started to dig at the screws that held the padlock in place. One by one the little brass studs dropped into her hand and she felt a surge of excitement as the padlock and hasp came away completely.

'Good,' Harrison said. 'Well done, now come here. We need to discuss a plan of action.'

Ellie sat, shaking, on the edge of the bed and Harrison took her hands in his. He brought them up to his lips and kissed them. Something stirred in the pit of Ellie's stomach. She looked at the blood still seeping through Harrison's makeshift bandages and she looked around the cabin, trying to overcome the sheer hopelessness of their situation. She had to face facts. She was going to have to get out of the skylight and swim to the shore for help, she who had never been out of her depth in the sea before.

Even at the outside chance that she would make it, would Harrison still be alive by the time the coastguard got to him? Tears welled up and spilled down Ellie's cheeks. She suddenly couldn't bear to think that she was going to lose him again.

Harrison lifted his good arm and wiped her tears away gently with the flat of his thumb.

'You know I can't go,' he whispered gently as though reading her thoughts.

'It's all down to you, my love.'

Ellie nodded.

'I don't know if I can do it. I don't want to leave you.'

Harrison felt a lump in his throat and swallowed it back.

'What's under those bunks? Do they lift up?' he said. 'Any life jackets in there?'

Ellie gave a sniff and moved towards the bunk where she had been lying. She pulled up the thin mattress and lifted up the ply-board underneath using the finger holes. The locker was a couple of feet deep and contained some spare fenders, a coil of rope and miraculously, a spare life jacket. Ellie pulled it out and let the ply-board and mattress drop back into place.

Harrison's eyes were wide now.

'Excellent,' he said. 'Put it on.'

Ellie's heart was racing and she could feel it pulsating in her throat. She felt sick with the fear and excitement of what she had to do. With shaking hands she pulled the life jacket over her head and tied the straps round her body securely.

'Don't inflate it until you get into the water, Ellie. OK?'

With relief, he saw that it was a fairly new jacket, in good condition and it was equipped with two emergency flares inside a pocket on the front.

Harrison questioned Ellie about her father's boat.

'What's at the stern? Is there a ladder? Steps? We must be sure you can get off without the crew seeing you.'

Ellie was shaking even more now and her teeth were chattering.

'There's a board running right across the back, just above water level, for swimmers and divers to sit on, and a ladder,' she told him.

Harrison closed his eyes for a moment trying to visualise their escape plan.

'OK,' he said finally, 'you must open up the hatch just a fraction, look to see if anyone is looking back towards the stern. If it's clear you must quickly, but very quietly, push the hatch right back, haul yourself up on to the coach-roof. Then close the hatch. Someone might notice it. Then drop straight down the back on to the back-board. Sit on it and slide straight into the water and start swimming away from the boat. Remember, slide in, don't jump. You don't want to make a splash.'

'I can't believe this is happening,' Ellie said. 'I hope I can do it. I don't want to let you down.'

Using his good arm he pulled her towards him.

'Whatever happens, Ellie,' he said hoarsely, 'you'll never have done that.'

Despite how weak he felt, he kissed her with as much passion and emotion as he could muster. She wanted to close her eyes and just melt into him but the urgency she could feel transmitted from him and the immense danger they were in was totally overwhelming. The feelings she had for him gave her the strength she needed for this mission.

'Don't forget you have flares,' Harrison said. 'Wait until you see another boat. Then pull the top off, hold it away from your face, and pull the little cord.'

Ellie yanked off another piece of sheeting and stuffed it down inside her T-shirt so that she would have something to signal with. Then she stood on the bunk as she lifted up the sky-light and peered out on to the deck. The auto pilot was on and the cockpit was empty. This was it, her chance had come.

She blew a final kiss at Harrison.

'I love you, too,' she said as she pushed back the sky-light and just about managed to squeeze through the opening.

As she went to close the window down again she spied a bottle of water on its side on the coach roof. Knowing how dangerous it was to linger, she quickly picked it up and hurled it down the opening on to Harrison's bunk before she closed the light and disappeared over the stern.

She sat on the board well out of sight from the cockpit and said a silent prayer to herself before she took a deep breath and bravely slid into the Indian Ocean. The water was cold and the surface was choppy as she bobbed around for a few moments, then she turned and floated on her back as she watched the Calypso Mermaid drift farther and farther away from her.

As she turned back over on to her front she was confronted with an infinite expanse of murky dark water, not the beautiful clear turquoise sea that was found nearer the shore. Then she saw the distance between her and that shoreline. It was just a misty haze far off on the horizon. She'd never make it!

9

Tom and Kim scanned the dining-hall for Ellie at breakfast. It was half-past seven and Tom was frowning.

'She's always up first and waiting for me to go for breakfast,' he said.

Kim was less worried.

'She's on holiday. Maybe she decided to have a lie-in. I'm sure she'll join us later.'

Kim was still basking in the afterglow of their night together and didn't want to think about the other woman. She knew Tom had had a thing about Ellie and that it hadn't been reciprocated, but she was feeling vulnerable. She hoped Tom hadn't been attracted to her on the rebound from Ellie.

'I think I should just go and check on her,' Tom said. 'She did feel a bit ill yesterday.'

'That was sea-sickness,' Kim persisted. 'You can't follow her around all the time like this, Tom. She's a grown woman and she doesn't love you.'

'I know that. It's obviously Harrison she loves, and I'm glad, really, because now I've found you. So don't get jealous, but I just want to make sure she's OK, then we can get something to eat and go down to the beach for a swim. It is OK for you to have today off work as well, isn't it?'

'I'm sure it is, but listen, I'll go and phone Harrison and check if he minds. That's if he's back yet from Nairobi. You go and check Ellie and I'll meet you in the dining-room.'

Five minutes later, Tom was back with a slightly more concerned look on his face.

'Her door is open and there's no-one there! There's a chair knocked over on the floor and Ellie's bag and purse is just left open on the side. She'd never leave her room like that.'

Kim was frowning, too.

'Well, I've just spoken to Ernest and he said that Harrison phoned him late last night from Mombasa to say that something had come up and he was coming straight over here to see Ellie.'

They walked through the lounge together towards the reception. Vince was just walking into his office. They followed him and asked if he had seen either Harrison or Ellie.

'One of the security guards said Harrison turned up here in the early hours of the morning to see a lady,' he replied. 'His Land-Rover's not outside though. Maybe they went off somewhere early together. I've noticed there's been something going on between them.'

While they had been talking, a message had wound itself out of the fax machine on Vince's desk. Tom scratched his head and was about to say something else when suddenly Vince let out a yell.

'Oh, no!' he said. 'I don't believe it!'

Tom instinctively knew that it was

bad news. He leaped round the desk and Vince laid out three pieces of paper on the table. There were two photographs and a message from the Nairobi police. Their contact in the UK had scanned the wanted picture of Max Hooper into the computer and with the aid of technology had removed his stringy brown hair and droopy moustache and replaced it with a short, dyed-black hairstyle.

The new photo that stared up at them from the desk had been computer aged by twelve years and was now a clean-shaven, black-haired Ryder Leason. According to the note attached to it, there was no such person as Ryder Leason! He had no past and no fingerprints on record. Max Hooper on the other hand did. He was wanted for serious fraud and they were sending someone to interview Ryder in the morning. They suggested that Miss Britten didn't approach him until they got there.

'That's Cameo's fiancé,' Kim said

naïvely. 'What on earth is this all about? What's going on and what's it got to do with Ellie?'

Vince was agitated.

'My sister's about to marry a crook by the looks of things.'

'I'm not sure what's going on myself,' Tom said incredulously. 'Ellie hasn't mentioned anything to me, but whatever it is I've got a feeling it's not good.'

Vince picked up the pieces of paper and looked at them again.

'What on earth has Ryder been up to? Are these two men the same person?'

'I think the only way we are going to find out anything is by going down to Leason Marina,' Tom said.

'The police said not to approach him,' Kim warned.

'It says Ellie, not us. We'll take my car,' Vince said, stuffing the folded pieces of paper into his back pocket.

★ ★ ★

Ellie had been in the water for nearly an hour, armed only with a desperate resolve and a couple of distress flares. She kept swimming then resting every five minutes trying to conserve energy. She had never swum for this long in her life and it seemed like a hopeless effort. But she kept thanking her lucky stars that there had been a life jacket in the locker. She would never have made it otherwise. However, she didn't feel she was any closer to the shore than she had been an hour ago. She had no idea what the time was but judging by the sun she thought it must be about half past seven. How would she cope as the sun got higher in the sky?

She turned on her back and floated again. She thought she could still see the dot that was Calypso Mermaid on the horizon. During the first few minutes of her escape she kept expecting to see it come about and chase after her. She started swimming again, more like paddling with the cumbersome life jacket on, but it was her only life-line. Without it she would certainly sink as her strength weakened. She could hardly bear to think of all that expanse of water underneath her.

The caress of the early-morning sun warmed the top of her head and she rolled her tongue around her parched mouth trying to summon some saliva. How she wished she had taken a swig of the water in the bottle she had found. She managed a smile as she thought how relieved Harrison must have felt when he saw that flying in through the sky-light. She hoped it had made him feel a bit more comfortable.

Ellie's leg muscles were starting to get cramped. She realised how unfit she was but she must keep going, she told herself.

Luckily her desire to live was stronger than her desire to give in, even though her shoulders ached as she paddled on, eyes rivetted to the shoreline, willing it to get nearer.

A rogue wave broke near her and she accidentally took in a mouthful of salty water. She choked and coughed it up, then soldiered on determinedly.

I wonder if Tom has noticed I'm missing yet, she thought.

Meanwhile, back on shore, Vince was actually driving inside the gates of Leason Marina. He brought his car to a halt at the far end of the carpark nearest the harbour. He got out, followed by Tom and Kim and they looked about for Ryder or Cameo. There wasn't much activity at this time of the morning. As they walked along the wooden decking of the jetty a young boy was washing down the decks of one of the fishing cruisers with a hose.

'Is Ryder about?' Vince asked. 'Mr Leason?'

The boy just shrugged his shoulders and carried on what he was doing.

'I can't see Simba anywhere,' Kim said.

They were standing beside an empty berth between two large cruisers.

'It was here yesterday when we went

157

out,' Kim observed.

'Well, well, where has Ryder gone this early in the morning?' Vince said.

Tom suddenly bent down and picked up a small gold chain with a dolphin charm attached to it.

'This is Ellie's ankle bracelet,' he said, looking very worried.

'Maybe she lost it when you went sailing yesterday,' Vince suggested.

Kim was shaking her head.

'She was definitely wearing it yesterday afternoon, after we got back. You remember when she got bitten, when you were all looking at my pictures? She bent down to rub her ankle. I saw the chain.'

Vince and Tom just looked at each other. Before they had a chance to say anything more, they heard someone calling them.

'Yoohoo!'

Cameo was walking down the gangway on to the jetty towards them.

'What are you all doing here so early, and where's Simba?'

'That's just what we were wondering,' Vince said. 'Didn't Ryder tell you he was going out this morning?'

Cameo linked her arm through her brother's.

'He slept on the boat last night,' she replied. 'He doesn't always tell me where he is going.'

'Did you two have a row or something?' Tom asked. 'Does he often sleep on board?'

Cameo frowned at them, aware that something was up.

'He said he had some business to attend to and that he'd sleep on board so he didn't disturb me. What is this all about? Has something happened to him?'

'Ellie and Harrison have gone missing,' Kim told her.

'Well, Ryder hasn't anything to do with that. Why should you think that?' Cameo snapped crossly, pulling her arm out of Vince's and looking at him for an explanation.

Tom held up Ellie's ankle bracelet.

'This is Ellie's,' he said.

Cameo was angry now.

'Vince,' she queried, 'what are you trying to tell me? That Ellie was on board the boat last night with Ryder? He wouldn't cheat on me.'

She started nervously, chewing on the side of her lip.

'She could have lost that when she was here yesterday.'

They all stared at her.

'No! I know it can't be true,' she insisted.

'We think it's worse than that, I'm afraid,' Vince said and handed his young sister the pages he had received from the Nairobi police.

Cameo looked at them in disbelief, shaking her head miserably and burst into floods of tears. Vince put his arm around her.

'I'm so sorry,' he said feebly. 'I don't think he's who he says he is, my love. He's fooled us all.'

'I can't believe it's true,' Cameo sobbed. 'There must be some mistake.'

'Let's go back up to the bungalow,' Vince said. 'We'll use the phone there.'

A bewildered Cameo followed the others as they walked away from the harbour and made their way towards the low white building. As they neared it, Vince frowned and looked over at a large shape covered with a tarpaulin at the side of the property.

'What's that, Cameo?' he asked.

She stopped sobbing long enough to shake her head at him.

'I don't know.'

Tom followed Vince over to it and Kim gasped as they pulled off the tarpaulin to reveal Harrison's Land-Rover hidden beneath it.

Inside the building, Kim took Cameo through to the lounge and sat her down. She picked up a box of tissues and pulled out a handful and gave them to the distraught woman. Meanwhile, Vince was on the phone to the coastguard. Kim and Tom both heard him giving them all the details of the yacht, its wanted skipper, and the fax they had received from Nairobi.

As he began to tell them about Ellie's and Harrison's disappearance and his concern about their safety, Kim and Tom both looked at each other, unable to put into words their feelings. The situation seemed so bizarre.

Vince put down the phone.

'They're on to it.'

'We can't just sit here and do nothing,' Tom said. 'There must be some way we can help.'

Vince agreed with him.

'You're right. We'll take one of the fast cruisers. If we open her right up we might be able to catch them up.'

Tom jumped up.

'Kim, will you stay here with Cameo? She's had a nasty shock.'

Kim nodded.

'Sure, you get off. But listen, when I phoned Ernest he said that Harrison would have got the hotel at about three this morning.'

Vince and Tom wasted no more time. It was now quarter past eight. Over five hours had elapsed. They had some catching up to do. They rushed down to the marina office and Vince picked some keys off the board. He checked the name tag on it with a smile.

'The Sapphire,' he said smugly. 'Now, she is fast.'

★ ★ ★

The sun had been beating down on Ellie's head for several hours and with a sickening dread she realised that the sun could kill her if she was out here for any length of time. She remembered the piece of sheet she had tucked into her T-shirt for a signal and floated on her back while she retrieved it. She managed to fold it into a triangle and tied it around her head.

It may help for a while, she thought.

She mustn't give in, she had to just hang in there. To surrender now would be suicide and it would mean certain death for Harrison. She could hardly bear to think of what was happening on the yacht. It had disappeared from her sight completely and she might never see him alive again. She choked back another tear and scanned the horizon again for a fishing boat or something. The flares were still tucked away in their pocket. Ellie prayed that they weren't waterlogged.

Meanwhile, unknown to her, Vince was being proved right — the Sapphire was fast. Fully fuelled, he motored out of the creek and the engine gave a throaty roar as he let the throttle out full. The waves crashed against the hull as they thudded over them and headed out to open sea.

Tom held a pair of binoculars up to his eyes and held on tightly to the safety rail as he turned to scan the horizon for the twin-masted ketch, ignoring his queasy stomach as the cruiser rose and fell in the early morning swell.

It was a race against time and they had no idea if they would win.

10

'Simba isn't the fastest of yachts,' Vince called out to Tom above the roar of the Sapphire's twin-engines. 'We might be able to catch up with them in this monster. Can you see anything yet?'

'A few fishing boats. No sign of any coastguards,' Tom replied as the bow rose again and slammed down into the waves.

He was having great trouble trying to focus his eyes through the binoculars while they were going up and down at such a rate.

'The coastguards will probably come from farther down towards Mombasa.'

'I hope one of us makes it,' Tom stated.

In his mind he was hoping that the coastguard would make it before them. They were only armed with a flare gun and a spear-gun, and Tom didn't think the two of them had much chance of storming the yacht on their own. Vince was all fired up and seemed up for anything, but they had to face facts. This was a serious situation and two people's lives were in real danger.

Out at sea, Ellie's strength had really begun to fade. Without the life jacket she knew she would have sunk by now. Tears stung the backs of her eyes and her breath was coming in short gasps. The thought of marauding sharks now plagued her and she had visions of her mutilated remains being washed up on the shore just as her parents had been found. Her limbs felt heavy and numb, her face encrusted with dried salt already and she could feel the sun had caught her cheeks and was still heating up her head despite the cloth wrapped around it.

Her eyes were blurring. Was she seeing things? She squinted and concentrated her vision on the horizon. She could see two fishing dhows in the distance and something much faster, bigger and more modern heading straight out to sea with a real purpose. It definitely wasn't a twin-masted ketch and Ellie didn't stop to think that it might be someone else working for Ryder.

She fumbled in the pocket of her life jacket for one of the flares and, remembering Harrison's instructions, she carefully took off the top with her numb and sea-wrinkled fingers. As she pulled the red taper, the inside of the flare shot up into the air and exploded into a ball of very bright light. She watched the vessels in the distance. Had they seen it? The dhows stayed where they were, but the other boat changed direction and started coming straight at her!

Ellie took the piece of sheet off her head and held it, ready to wave. If the crew were looking for a boat in distress they might run her down!

It felt like hours before the boat was upon her. She waved her makeshift flag for all she was worth and relief flooded through her as the boat appeared to have spotted her and was slowing down. Then Tom's face looked over the side at her in sheer amazement.

'Ellie! Good heavens! What on earth happened? Here grab this!'

He threw her the life ring.

Vince had put the engine into neutral. There was silence as they bobbed about on the surface, and the two men leaned over the side and grabbed the straps of the life jacket and hauled Ellie aboard as she hung for dear life on to the life ring. She was shaking so much she could barely speak as they helped her into the cockpit.

Tom fetched a bottle of water and a blanket and they threw questions at her as she drank greedily and pulled the blanket round her as her body broke out in a convulsion of shivers.

'Ellie, what happened? Can you tell us? Where is Harrison? Are you OK?'

At last she spoke.

'I'm OK, I think, just exhausted. Thank goodness you found me. I've been in the water for hours and I didn't seem to be getting any closer to land.'

She looked back out to sea, fretting and breathing hard.

'Harrison! You've got to help him. He's been shot.'

She tried to stand up but Tom pushed her down again gently.

'Sit down, Ellie. Don't worry. The coastguards are on their way. They know all about Ryder and who he really is.'

'It might be too late!' she said hysterically. 'He might die. Oh, please, don't let him die,' she sobbed.

Vince started up the engine again.

'We won't let him die,' he promised, hoping that they would be able to do something. 'But, tell me, how did you get mixed up in all this, anyway? I don't understand.'

Tom had his arms around Ellie trying to comfort her and stop her from shaking.

'Max Hooper,' she started. 'He embezzled money from my parents' company. He was my dad's accountant. I think he . . . I think he killed them.'

Ellie proceeded to explain to Tom and Vince how her suspicions first arose with Cameo's locket, and how she had then thought she had recognised Ryder. She finished by telling them the drama of the previous night and how she escaped from the boat.

'It's unbelievable. Like a gangster movie,' Vince said.

When Ellie went on to explain how the yacht, Simba, was really her parents' boat, Calypso Mermaid, Tom gave a low whistle.

'How come all this was going on and I didn't know?' he asked Ellie.

'I think you've been a bit preoccupied these past few days.'

Ellie managed a slight smile despite the gravity of their situation.

Tom had the decency to blush.

'Well, I'm not one to let the grass grow under my feet. Anyway, are you feeling a bit better? I think you should go inside and lie down.'

'Shall we go now?' Vince asked, and pushed the gear lever forward.

The engine growled again and they were off. Down below, Tom helped Ellie out of her wet clothes and found a spare T-shirt and shorts left behind by one of the fishing holiday-makers for her to put on.

He laid her down on the saloon seat inside the cabin and found more dry blankets. He rolled one into a pillow shape and tucked it under her head.

'Rest now,' he told her. 'I'm going back up top to keep a look-out. Try not to worry. We'll get him.'

There was nothing else Ellie could do now to help Harrison except pray. It was in the hands of Vince, Tom and the coastguards. She was exhausted and found it impossible to stay awake.

It was a long while later when she awoke to the sounds of shouting and other boat engines nearby. She tried to raise her head, her whole body like a lead weight. She looked out of the porthole. They were idling just off the stern of Calypso Mermaid and Ellie could see two coastguard boats and men in uniforms carrying guns.

As she watched, hardly daring to breathe, she saw Ryder transferred to one of the boats, in handcuffs. Her heart started to beat faster. There were so many armed police swarming over the yacht it was difficult to see exactly what was going on. Then her heart missed a beat as she saw a stretcher being manhandled out of the stern cabin by four strong men.

Her hand flew to her mouth as she gasped.

'Oh, Harrison! Please be all right. Please.'

Vince was worn out from standing at the helm for so many hours, so Tom took over steering and they followed the coastguard vessels back to the mainland and Mombasa so that Harrison could be transferred to hospital there. Vince went down into the cabin and started making coffee in the tiny little galley area.

Ellie looked hopefully at him, frightened to ask how Harrison was, but needing to know all the same.

'He's badly hurt, Ellie,' Vince told her, not wanting to get her hopes up too much in case the worse happened and he didn't make it. 'He's strong though. I hope he pulls through, for your sake. You really love him, don't you?' he said as he spooned the coffee into the mugs. 'Tom said you and Harrison had something going years ago.'

'Yes, we did. I still don't really know what happened then. But I'm not going to lose him again. I know that much.'

Vince nodded his head and truly hoped she wouldn't have to.

* * *

Vince walked through the swing doors and went and sat back down next to Ellie and Tom on the benches of the hospital waiting-room.

'Did you get through?' Tom asked,

stretching his legs out in front of him.

Vince had been to phone Cameo and Kim to let them know what was happening.

'I did. All's well. Cameo's been sedated and is sleeping now. Kim is dying to know what has happened but I just gave her the rough details.'

Tom sighed. It had been a long day and Harrison had been in surgery for some time now. There should be some news soon. Ellie had been checked over and given a clean bill of health and now she sat quietly staring ahead.

She was instantly alert, however, as a nurse came through the doors towards them. They all stood up, searching her face for signs of good news.

'How is he?' Ellie said.

She thought she was prepared for the worst but as the nurse opened her mouth to speak she realised she wasn't at all, and tears started to roll down her cheeks. The nurse smiled.

'It's OK. The operation went well,' she informed her. 'We got the bullet out. He's very weak but he's going to be OK.'

Ellie's tears turned to tears of joy.

'Oh, thank you . . . thank you so much. May I see him?'

'Not all of you at once,' she told them.

Vince and Tom just grinned at her.

'Go on,' Tom said.

'Yeah, off you go. Give him our best.'

Ellie opened the door and quietly slipped in. Harrison was surrounded by drips and machines but he was breathing steadily.

'Harrison,' she whispered, 'it's Ellie. Can you hear me? You're in hospital.'

He opened his eyes and looked up at her, a smile creeping over his face.

'I knew you could do it. You saved my life,' he said hoarsely.

'Just in time by the looks of things. I was so frightened.'

She picked up his hand and held it.

'Harrison, don't you ever scare me like that again. Promise?'

'You're obviously going to be staying

around me then, to want me to give you that undertaking.'

'If you beg me to, I might think about it.'

'How about if I just asked you to marry me?'

* * *

The waiter put the drinks down in front of them. Ellie was frowning.

'Harrison, what really happened ten years ago when you walked out on me? You said it was complicated, but I never understood.'

Harrison was wearing a sling and winced as he leaned forward and picked up his glass with his good arm.

'I was going to tell you when I got back from Nairobi but events rather took over. Your father,' Harrison began, 'found out about us. He wasn't happy. He knew I was a bit of a globetrotter and he thought that you would give up the career you wanted in publishing to come round the world with me and would regret it later. He was worried that you hadn't had any other boy-friends your own age and he was just concerned that you were making a big mistake.'

'He told you that? And you never said anything?'

'Yes. He warned me off, basically. I mean, I was quite a bit older than you and we'd known each other all our lives, since we were small. Roger thought you loved me more as an older brother, that you were confusing your feelings. He did it for all the right reasons, Ellie. I suppose I was weak but I also respected him too much to disregard what he was saying.'

Ellie fingered the mermaid locket around her neck. Cameo had given it back to her when she had found out where it had come from.

'Well,' she said, shaking her head, 'I was his only child. He must have cared a great deal about my welfare to do that.'

'Can you forgive us both?'

Ellie smiled.

'Nothing to forgive. But we've got a lot of catching up to do,' she said with a loving wink.

THE END